COST OF SURVIVAL

Book #1
Worth of Souls series

By
B.R. Paulson

B. R. PAULSON

COST OF SURVIVAL

Captiva Publishing
www.brpaulson.com

Cover design – Ashley Byland from Redbird Designs.
Editing by Grammar Smith Editing

B. R. PAULSON

ACKNOWLEDGEMENTS

Brian – Nothing more to say… but I love you.

Jill, Shelley, and Brooklyn – Thanks for your support. This book grew because of you.

Kammie – Thanks for catching the important stuff.

Mandie – Thank you… I can't even list everything you do.

Survivors – Thank you for requesting another apocalypse-style story from me. I hope you love it as much as I do!

B. R. PAULSON

CHAPTER 1

Huge earthquakes didn't happen in the northwest. The ground shook anyway and I grabbed the sink to avoid falling over.

My image wavered in the mirror and I focused on my white knuckles as I braced myself for stability.

I squeezed my eyes shut, fear shooting through me. My breathing hitched. Warned that hysteria comes on quickly, I lifted my gaze and pierced my image with a glare. "Get your crap together, Kelly. This isn't a surprise." I narrowed my eyes for good measure, in case I wasn't taking myself seriously.

Slowing my breathing, I ignored my racing pulse. Nothing I could do about that.

Great, every fear my mother ever warned me about was coming to fruition. There'd be no living with her now. My fingers slipped over the cool ceramic as the shaking slowed, but didn't stop.

From outside the small high-up windows, screams of other people started low and sporadic but increased in frequency and volume.

Protected by thick tiled walls in the girls' bathroom, I turned off the water and wiped my damp hands down the front of my green shirt, leaving dark wet prints on the cotton.

Class had been in session when I'd taken the hall pass to get some air, leaving the rest of the bathroom empty. With all the muffled noise outside the room, I didn't remember a time I felt so alone.

And I didn't want to leave.

Another rumble sent the building into a spasm. A large crack spread across the ceiling, sprinkling dust into my pseudo-safe space. I sneezed, rubbing at the gritty particles powdering my skin.

Yanking open the door, I stopped and gasped. I should've stayed in the bathroom.

Kids ran, screaming and crying, toward the front doors or rather where the front doors used to be. The whole wall had disappeared.

Where the double-glass doors had manned the entrance of my high school, a large gaping hole let the late spring sunlight in mixed with dust and smoke. Twisted metal and mauled concrete gaped with angry jagged edges. The scent of burning wood and singed skin drifted on the rounded smoke clouds.

Breathe, Kelly, just breathe. But I didn't want to. Breathing hurt. The smoke and ash in the air had a taste and scent I instinctively did not want in my body. I lifted my t-shirt collar and held the cotton over my nose.

No matter what, I couldn't force my other hand to let go of the door frame. My fingers tightened and I stared. My eyes watered under the onslaught of smoke. The breeze outside might as well be nonexistent. The smoke and dust refused to clear.

Come on. I blinked, scanning the interior of the school hallway.

Bodey. Where was Bodey? He was supposed to be at the school for a track meeting. He had graduated the year and came in to help out with coaching and to train for track at the college. Had he made it to the gym? Or anywhere?

A girl dashed into my line of sight. Cyndi. Someone I recognized – *focus on her*.

I reluctantly released the frame and waved my hand at a girl I usually ate at the same table with. We weren't friends – exactly – but in the immediate chaos, even lunch acquaintances were better than nothing.

"Cyndi! Over here!" Not that being with me was safer by any means, but at least I wouldn't be alone and, with a shaky movement to her hands, she probably could use someone to stand with for a minute too.

Wild-eyed, she paused in her jagged scrambling through people toward the missing front door and her gaze fell on me. Recognition smoothed her jitters and she bee-lined for my spot, ducking and swerving around other screaming students.

As she approached, her screams died down, replaced by some kind of a whimpering moan. She looked left and right, behind her, back at me, like I was an anchor to help her get to one spot for security.

Finally a part in the smoke revealed a glimpse of the blue sky dotted with black items. A shrill whistle announced another explosion across the street in the new subdivision. I ducked.

The ground moved, but not as distinctly as when I was in the restroom. A hole in the cloud got bigger, framing clear sky filled with big and small black shapes moving over the land.

I squinted. With eyes watering, I couldn't trust my vision – or any of my senses. Everything was off. Just like Mom had said this would play out.

She'd warned me. Continually. No matter how well she and her friends had prepared, nothing stopped the events from happening.

Not the pandemic and the eradication of more than two-thirds of the world's population – we were learning about the 'end of conservative man' in Senior History. Did two years in the past count as history?

My mom's co-op couldn't prevent any of the loss. The number of the group went from over fifty to nineteen. For all their preparations and praying, more than half disappeared because of the disease.

Even Mom's preparations didn't keep us from losing my dad and brother. To the same horrible disease. Or the rest of our family on the east coast. Everyone was gone. So many bodies, towns gave up trying to have official burials. Most of the dead went into mass graves or were burned.

I can't imagine what the less developed countries went through.

The bigger, more developed countries didn't even get hit as bad as those *other worlds*.

Another black torpedo-shaped body fell closer to a building on the other side of the street. The explosion rocked the ground.

Cyndi squeaked and the students around us ducked into a spastic type of bear crawl with their hands on the ground and butts at half-crouch.

I'm not sure what annoyed me more, the fact I hadn't dodged anything or that I hadn't started running home, like Mom had drummed into me with my training.

Why was I so afraid to call the black things what they were?

Bombs.

Bombs. *Say it out loud, Kelly.* "Bombs." Did my effort count in a whisper?

"I can't believe they're bombing us!" Of course Cyndi could say the word. She ran before I did, too.

She reached for my arm, panting and desperate. "Kelly, I need to get to the elementary school. Bobby's over there and he's probably so scared." Her younger brother had the entire third grade wrapped around his finger. With his charm, he could run the world one day.

Nothing made more sense than searching for your loved ones, but with bombs detonating left and right, the last thing I needed involved watching a partial-friend blow to pieces. I motioned toward the teachers and students whizzing past us with no real direction. "Wait a minute and then head over. I'm sure he's fi—"

A bomb caught my attention. The direction and speed as it fell from the sky sent a chill along my hair line.

I grabbed Cyndi and shoved her into the bathroom, against the wall. "Get down!" My scream sliced through the air and she dropped to the ground, copying my movement of arms over my head and face tucked to my knees.

Closer than the house explosions, that one thundered underground until queasiness roiled in my stomach. Solid, consuming fear finally found me. I don't know where it went hiding, but holy cow, vomit wanted to be found, too.

I didn't want to see what had happened.

Cyndi raised her head. "What was *that*?" Her screech ended on a sob.

I could look. I didn't want to, but I made myself. Knowledge is power, or so Mom always said.

Glancing out the door and through the hole where the entrance had been, I tried shutting out the horror before me. I gathered as many details as I could to help Cyndi in some way.

The door didn't close easily. I turned back to the girl who desperately needed a friend. How did I soften my words without crying? "The elementary school."

Her eyes widened. She jumped to pull open the door. Stepping out into the hallway, she stared at the black, smoking and burning mess that had – moments before – housed her little brother and hundreds of other children.

Shock froze her mouth open. She didn't even acknowledge the other witnesses jostling around her, trying to find their own chaos controller.

Cyndi didn't respond. She didn't make a sound. I'm not even sure she breathed.

As if on autopilot, Cyndi stepped forward until she ran into the pile of rubble marking the school explosion site. She didn't let anything get in her way. Bending down on all fours, she climbed over the debris in a straight line toward the elementary.

To my horror, I didn't stop her.

Why would I? What would I do? Tell her not to go? Tell her she would be safer in the high school? Psh. I couldn't guarantee anything for her – for anyone. Nothing about World War III was predictable. Most importantly, though, I could understand nothing would keep me away from my brother, if he'd been in that school.

I scanned the scene being slowly revealed by the departing smoke. How far would I be able to see once the debris had completely cleared?

Four blocks from the elementary school, my home should be easy to get to. Had the houses between the schools and my backyard been wiped out by bombs? Fire?

The real question I didn't want to ask – didn't want the answer to – had my house been hit?

I swallowed, searching further. Could Bodey be out there?

Screams sound-tracked the drifting papers burning as they fell. Running boys and girls and the dazed teachers hanging onto the jagged edges of the building as they stumbled out to the grounds completed the scene.

My mom wouldn't scream. She prayed too hard to feel real fear. No, she would do the best with what she had.

True fear curdled in my stomach. If my house had been hit by a bomb, then Mom would be gone. As much as I fought with her, she was all I had left. I wasn't ready to lose her.

Every night my mom taught me about the arrival of World War III and its inevitability, what to expect, what not to accept, and how to stay safe.

According to Mom we would all lose the final war which was the only outcome no one could control. The information was right there, smack in the center of Revelations. She would quote more scriptures and I would try to retreat into my happy place where mothers didn't lecture their daughters on morality and religion.

A burning sting in my forearm brought my attention back to the chaos around me. Chunks of burning wood marked my flesh. I brushed them off, jerking my arms closer to my body.

Even the teachers ran with no real plan. Mr. Denning stood in the corner, feet from the entrance hole and muttered, walking two steps forward and stopping when he rammed his head into the wall.

I didn't have time to find Bodey. I had to find Mom.

My plan needed to be fast. Mom would expect me home as soon as possible. If she… I shook my head. Nope. One of the tactics Mom drilled into me was never think defeatist thoughts. If you give into the negativity, you're already defeated.

What did I need? Was there anything at the school I had to take with me? Fortunately, I wouldn't have to retrieve my backpack. My locker had disappeared in the mess destroyed by the front door. As a senior I had premium real estate by the entrance and that particular seniority right had cost me.

The few blocks would pass quickly. I just needed to get going. I shut out the fear sending tingles to my toes that she wouldn't be there when I got home or even that I might not make it home.

I had to get home. There were no other options.

Darting into the mass exodus of teachers and students, I stumbled over the rocks and broken glass before finding my footing in the deceptively green grass.

Nothing could get in my way.

A younger boy – maybe a freshman? – grabbed at my arm. His fingers had a charred-hot-dog-on-a-stick look with the flesh plump and oozing with blackened tips. "Help me," he sobbed, blood seeping slowly from his nose and ears.

I reached for him, desperate to hold him up, give him some form of relief. Grabbing his forearms above where the material had melted to his skin, I tried holding him up. I tried.

His face froze and the focused pain in his eyes faded. Right there in my arms. He died. And I didn't... I gasped. I couldn't hold onto his sudden weight on my hands and he fell to the ground, drooping over rebar protruding from the mangled concrete beside us.

Backing up, I covered my mouth. Someone bumped me from behind.

I blew air out of my lungs. *Calm down, Kelly. You can do this. Get it together.*

A teacher blew a whistle and heads turned. They'd been forcing dumb drills on us for the past few months now. Rumors the "war to end all wars" was right around the corner spread like gossip in a high school.

Everyone became survival experts.

Via the drill, a teacher would whistle and all the students would surround the leader. Everyone was supposed to wait patiently for help or seek shelter together.

Always together. Like they – whoever *they* were – didn't trust any *one* person out by themselves.

Maybe Mom had learned how to telepathically transfer her conspiracy theories into my mind. I swear, it wouldn't be the first time.

Fear that Bodey had arrived in town filled me but I focused on the task at hand.

Big groups were a bad idea. More people made bigger targets. Glancing at the body of the boy one last time, I broke into a loose jog and forced myself not to sprint. I had to hold the same calm pace so I could see all my options ahead of me.

People who panicked died.

Another Mother-ism.

Yet I would listen, because for once? Mother just might be right.

B. R. PAULSON

CHAPTER 2

Cars and trucks crawled by me. So close together I could pretend the vehicles were attached by string and pulled by a large child, maybe a large toddler throwing a temper tantrum.

I dodged between a sedan and a pickup, the drivers hollering from their windows at groups of children. I'm not sure about their execution, but I'm glad they put a stall on the string of careening vehicles blocking my way.

In a fenced subdivision beside the sidewalk where I jogged, another explosion crashed through the air, shaking the ground. I dove to the grass, banging my knee on a partially hidden sprinkler head. "Oomph!"

Rolling to the side, I grabbed my leg and stared upward.

Numerous black and grey plumes of smoke dirtied the clear blue sky. I didn't want to blow apart and become a whiff of smoke. Not today.

Time between explosions increased. The number of dark shapes in the sky lessened, but didn't disappear. Peering through stray tendrils of smoke and floating debris, I could just make out the outline of my neighborhood. Everything appeared to be intact – so far.

Pushing up to stand, I shook off the ache below my kneecap. I would definitely bruise, but what if it swelled? Injuries to the knees could impede running. Lovely, just what I wanted when I already watched people die and buildings explode.

I didn't *want* to look behind me, but I couldn't fight the urge. I was like the rubber-necking fools at a bad highway accident.

Multi-colored shirts marked a large group of people gathered at the north end of the parking lot.

More cars stopped on the road and people jumped out of their doors. Random stopping and starting while they searched only created more of a traffic problem. Arms waving and voices raised in desperation, they worked to claim someone in the crowd or maybe to find someone who wasn't there anymore.

The dead boy's fear-filled face crossed my mind and I squeezed my eyes shut for the briefest second.

I turned forward, waving the caustic air from my face. Moving the smoke around didn't help. In fact, I might have made things worse since little particles of ash coated my tongue and throat.

My house still stood. *Oh thank the heavens.* Relief loosened the tension in my muscles and my stride steadied while my shoulders dropped to a comfortable position.

The immediate houses around ours had escaped damage but the next street over had nothing standing except an old oak tree I had climbed once as a small girl. Dwelling on the damage and the memories wouldn't get me home any faster.

A piercing whistle drew my gaze as I jogged. My mom waved from our back deck. I coughed, lifting my hand to return the wave.

I squinted. Was she holding a tea mug? Did she think the queen was coming or something? I picked up my pace, lengthening my stride. There were getting bombed and my mother had a cup of tea.

Rolling my eyes, I sprinted the last hundred feet across the road, dodging cars and panicked people carrying boxes from their homes.

The acrid scent of burnt hair and flesh hit me at the same time I stumbled. Looking down, I recoiled, gagging deep in my throat.

What was—

Hand to my mouth, I held in my sob. My brother's dog, Captain Pete, had somehow been burned – horribly. He whimpered, scratching himself closer to the open gate.

I had forgotten to close the stupid gate on my way to school. Captain Pete had gotten out because of me. Hot tears coursed my cheeks and I clenched my teeth together. He stopped moving and his eyes closed.

Oh, no. Twice? In less than an hour? *No. Please, no.*

Standing, I sobbed and backed through the open gate. I couldn't slam it shut. My increased speed combined with the discovery of Captain Pete left me huffing. Chemical-tinged smoke burned my throat as I gasped through my mouth. Breathing through my nose hurt worse.

I stamped down my hysteria. Fear wanted to boil over. I had to pull my stuff together. Mom would not tolerate panic. She wouldn't accept anything from me that we hadn't practiced. She was nothing, if not prepared.

Stopping at the corner of the house, I leaned against the shaded vinyl siding.

Mom was okay. Captain Pete and that kid weren't. Half the school wasn't and judging by the damage in the neighborhood half the community wasn't either.

But Mom was. She was so *fine*, she took time to make and enjoy a cup of tea.

"Kelly? Come on. Get up here." Mom called me as if I was just getting in from hanging out with friends. Where was her panic? Her fear? Of course I wouldn't be allowed to witness them. She would bury them beneath her faith, drown them in her tea. If she even had any emotions like that at all.

I clamped my mouth shut. That wasn't fair. Mom cared about me. She had more empathy than most people. She didn't overreact to situations because of her faith. Blaming her for events outside of her control wouldn't sort anything out or make the world safer.

Pasting a neutral expression on my face, I bit back my fear. If she looked too closely, she'd see my hands shaking. I reached for the thin gold chain my dad had given me before... well, I didn't want to think about *that* or my neutral expression would fade.

"Hey, Mom. What do you think?" How unnatural to be blasé about the horror around us.

But she expected control. She expected faith. We had a plan and we would follow the steps.

She sipped her tea, focusing her eyes over the cup rim toward the deteriorating garden of houses spread every direction around our place.

The explosions had all but ended. Dark eyebrows arched over eyes so blue she often styled her brown hair back from her face to enhance them. "Well, this certainly isn't a drill, Kelly. Grab your father's bug out bag and your hiking boots and meet me in the kitchen. We need to make some sandwiches and grab some fresh food before we leave."

I climbed the stairs two at a time, holding onto the railing, and stopped inches from my mom. She didn't drag her attention from the tragedy around us. Turning to see where I'd escaped, I clenched my hands at my sides. "We have MREs in the bags. Do we really need to pack more stuff? And why Dad's?" Not that I was really complaining. Something of his would go with me wherever I went. A plan I could get on board with pretty quick.

Plus, I just needed to talk about anything mundane, anything to keep my mind off the last sixty minutes of my life.

"Because I readjusted the bag's contents. The majority of your stuff is in there, his bag is bigger, and can carry more." She sighed, turning toward me and lifting her mug. "And we're taking as much fresh food as we can because I paid for it and I hate to see it go to waste. Okay?" She narrowed her eyes and I caught a glimpse of fear she didn't want me to see.

I nodded. "Yes, ma'am." Stomping wouldn't behoove me. She would just make me walk the path again. I reined in my frustration and bit my tongue – not hard enough to draw blood but with enough force the sting dulled my anger. She didn't ask how the people at school were handling the attacks. She didn't asking anything, but issued orders instead.

Her gaze slid downward, taking in my arms and the blackened soot over the tops of the forearms. "You're burned. Is it bad?"

Shrugging, I waited for her to examine my skin. As a nurse, she had more sense than most people did and a little bit of burning wouldn't faze her – even on me.

A large part of me didn't care where or what we did and, in fact, the weightlessness of allowing my mom to plan and control everything released some of the stress of the moment.

If everything went down the way my mom claimed, I would never see my home again. The pictures on the walls, the miniatures claiming the shelves, everything we collected over our lives would be left behind. Even the small personal items of Braden's and my dad's. Nothing extra was allowed to go.

Once a few months ago, I asked Mom if I could fit something in my pocket, if it could go. She had stopped cutting onions and turned to study me. Eyes wet from the dicing, she pursed her lips before speaking slowly. "I'm not doing this to be mean, Kelly. Everything is planned out for a reason. Every ounce is calculated for survival. We might not even need any of it anyway. I'm sure we'll be fine."

I had nodded, turning back to setting the table for the two of us. We would need it, but neither of us wanted to call out the fallacy of her statement right then. Why would we? Pressure mounted all over the world and many times we pretended we didn't notice.

The only items allowed would be the ones I could fit in my pack. How depressing. No tablet or music or teddy bear. Nothing extra.

She couldn't understand my bitterness.

Upstairs in my room, I could almost pretend nothing was happening. Like I'd just gotten home from school and Mom had cookies in the oven or something.

Waiting for me on my comforter my dad's bug out bag sat beside my emptied maroon bag.

She had transferred everything for me. Not one thing had been left behind. Her methods sometimes sucked in how she dealt with me, but with that act, she proved that she *got* me. She didn't question why most of my stuff was gender neutral or leaned toward the more masculine side.

The space! She hadn't been kidding. The top third sagged with emptiness, which would be used for food, not my favorite books or my jewelry box handmade by my dad when I turned six. Everything would stay.

I knew the drill. We were lucky in this scenario. I had time to change and time to pack appropriately. Based on Mom's lack of pacing, I sensed we weren't leaving in the next five minutes which surprised me.

According to Mom's explanations, I'd be missing out on showers for quite a while, which I didn't find funny, but I understood. What I hadn't quite figured out was why she wanted my chest flattened with three sports bras and an ace bandage.

Yet, I complied, the tight material compressing my ribcage and decreasing my ability to inhale comfortably.

After replacing my jeans, green shirt, and normal bra with dark cargo pants, three sports bras, a black thermal long sleeve shirt under a lightweight but warm t-shirt, I brushed my hair and pulled the strands into a tight braid.

Yanking on my hiking boots, I glanced around my room one last time. My stomach hurt with the reality of what was happening. Everything my mother had ever warned me about jumped forward into reality.

She'd been right. I didn't want her to be right.

Mostly though, I didn't want to believe it.

I pulled the bag onto my back and paused at the doorway. Rubbing the foot of a small teddy bear I had since my third Christmas, I looked at my bed. Then at my things, at the evidence of *me* – of what made my life, made me who I had become.

Would I lose that girl? Would my mother's predictions continue to settle on the correct side of the spectrum?

I shut the door softly. I could hold tight to the illusion that my room wouldn't change, it would stay unmolested and I could return one day.

My heart sank. I would never be there again. I wasn't stupid. Hopeful, yes. Stupid, not so much.

"Kelly?" Mom's voice broke my reverie.

"Yep, coming." I clomped down the steps and joined her in the kitchen. She'd changed in the small amount of time I'd been gone and her bag stood patiently on the table, waiting for more items.

Bread and cheese covered the table. "Mom, there has to be enough here for thirty sandwiches." I shook my head. What would we do with so much food?

"Eighteen actually. Trust me, we'll be grateful we have it tomorrow or the next day." She cut more cheese, laying the slices across the bread. Nodding toward the mayonnaise container, she added. "Get going, please. I'm sure the looting will start soon. I want to be out of here before the real danger reaches the neighborhoods." She slid baggies from the bright blue box and set one beside each sandwich.

Looting and rioting. I focused on spreading the mayonnaise and the mustard.

Once complete, each sandwich went into a separate baggie and Mom stuffed those into one of our bags. "I'm short two sandwich baggies. Let's eat one now." She retrieved plates from the cabinets for us and gently set our sandwiches on the shiny cream ceramic.

To be honest, it had never occurred to me she would be missing *things*, too. I thought I was the only materialistic one.

Swiping a knife over the last bread, I peeked at her solemn face. "Are you scared, Mom?" Part of me waited as if frozen in anticipation – like everything hung on her answer. What if she said yes? Would real terror set in? What if she said no? Would I be able to trust her? Because who in their right mind wouldn't be scared in that exact second?

She tossed in oranges and apples, yogurts and even a bag of mini-marshmallows. "You know what? The situation is frightening, and yet, I can't help but be grateful for what we have. The steps we've taken to be prepared for this type of event. Scared? You bet. Is the fear debilitating? Nope. The Lord is on our side." She winked at me.

Throwing her faith into the mix answered the question perfectly. She was afraid but she didn't doubt we would be fine. Only my mom would find a way to answer the question and comfort me all at once.

A shot rang out a few houses down. Mom and I looked toward the front door and back at each other. Faith aside, my heart pounded.

Things just got real.

She dropped her voice into a muffled murmur. "Grab your coats and layer up. I don't know when we'll be able to stop." She pointed at the chair where my jackets hung and she pulled on her own layers. I followed suit. What else was I supposed to do?

A new urgency fueled our movements.

Pushing at the tops of our bags, she clicked them closed and hefted mine onto my back.

"Oh, wow." Adjusting my shoulders, I shrugged at the pressure of the bag.

She paused, turning to me and rubbing my shoulder. Mom ducked and met my gaze. "I know. I'm sorry."

Her apology scared me more than any of the bombs or the screams of people emerging from fiery homes, or even the fact that I'd be leaving the relative safety of my life-long home. Because my mom didn't apologize for things, especially stuff outside her control. At least to me.

We grabbed our sandwiches and I followed her without another sound. Who knew when I would have to apologize for my rudeness or complaints – I needed to learn to keep comments to myself. And I would. I just needed patience. Wasn't that supposed to be a virtue?

Late March daylight faded around six pm in the northern Idaho region. Streetlights that hadn't been blown to bits didn't flicker on. Instead they stood along the streets with their heads bent as if in mourning. Homes on fire lit up the neighborhood similar to overzealous bonfires seeking the stars.

Mom shut the back door. Her hand lingered an extra moment on the glass of the slider and she bowed her head. Probably to pray again. Another shot resounded off the neighborhood fences.

I ducked around, looking for the culprit or group of people. The sound was so close.

Her consistent praying made us late for anything and everything in our normal everyday activities. She was going to screw us over in the here and now.

"Are we taking the car?" Naturally, I whispered. Undue attention wouldn't be good with people already shooting in our neighborhood.

She shook her head. "No. Too conspicuous and we would only get so far. With gas at six dollars for so long, I haven't filled up the tank in a while." Mom led the way down the steps to the backyard. "We're going up through the new construction sites. Shouldn't be anyone that way just yet and if we need to we can camp the night there."

"Why don't we sleep here tonight? The looting shouldn't reach us until morning, right?" I glanced up where my bedroom window would be, already missing the soft mattress and squishy pillow. But the shots had been too close and I was really just begging for the chance to cling a teeny bit more to what we had to leave behind us.

Mom lowered her head and then lifted it again. She didn't look back at me. "Do you really want to take that chance?"

I couldn't give her an honest answer. I didn't know what chance exactly I would be taking, but I could tell her I didn't want to find myself in any of the situations she had described as possibilities over the years.

Not one of those scenarios had occurred in our house. I could pretend our house was magic and we'd be safe forever there.

Or Mom couldn't see herself living in a home where bad things happened. That was more likely and easier to swallow.

Who wouldn't want to believe the good or even the improbable good? Especially since Dad and Braden had been safe and protected at home until they had gone together on a business trip to Atlanta, Georgia.

Their illness and death had occurred away from home. We had never gotten an answer regarding the disease – too many had died, too many to bury. Too many...

I didn't want to think of my dad and my little brother. Not right then. Not when I walked away from their memories.

What were we doing? Were we so desperate to survive we would abandon everything?

World War III couldn't be all bad. Humanity wouldn't change so much we wouldn't be safe with other people.

Right?

CHAPTER 3

Trudging down the empty sidewalk, I focused on placing one foot and then another in the shadow of my mother's steps. The further from town we walked, the more deserted the streets and houses seemed.

To our right, the grating sound of metal rolling on metal scratched through the smoky air.

Mom grabbed my sweatshirt and shoved me behind a privacy line of arborvitae. The scratchy branches and foliage clung to strands of my hair, freeing them from my braid. She tucked me between her and the tall bushes. Through thin slits we watched in half-hunkered down positions.

In the setting daylight, a man poked his head from the open garage. He checked the road, left and right, inspecting homes and their yards. For the briefest moment, I could've sworn he spied us, but his gaze moved on. After another heartbeat, he disappeared back inside his garage.

Red lights glowed from the opening at the same time growls from a turned-over engine reached us.

"Get down on the ground." Mom pushed on my shoulder, and I sank to the short grass under the pressure. She joined me, yanking at the dark hood on my jacket to cover my face. "He's going to come this way. We came in the only entrance by road." She really had researched our route.

The two-door Jeep backed down the driveway and turned around on the street. He passed us, things tied to the tops and back of the vehicle with bungee cords. Small faces peered into the neighborhood from the back windows and a woman's face blocked the man's in the passenger window.

Mom folded her arms. She murmured a quick prayer and stood once the red lights had turned the corner to the exit. "They won't make it far."

And that's all she said.

Real sadness welled within me. Would anyone else make *it*? Would we?

We tromped onto the sidewalk, falling easily into our pace. Mom looked around us consistently, as if knowing where we were and if anyone was around us would keep us safe.

The acrid scent of smoke didn't burn as badly so far north.

I snorted, watching as we passed line after line on the sidewalk.

Mom stopped and turned, panting slightly. The light wasn't lingering and shadows hollowed her cheeks and eyes. "What's the matter?"

Shaking my head, I planted my feet beside her. "Nothing's wrong. I was laughing at myself." Grateful for another break, I continued, trying to prolong the rest even if only for a few more seconds. "The smoke doesn't seem as thick up here. I think it's funny we haven't gone more than a couple miles and I'm already talking like we're so far away."

I bit back on confessing about the sting in my heart that I was leaving home. Mom had already prepared me for this. Inevitable and destined. Nothing much more was needed, I guess.

She glanced beyond me, toward town, eyes narrowed. "Yep, I can imagine that would be funny." Piercing me with her stare, she brushed at my sleeves and small white and black flakes smeared more than anything. "You have ash on your clothes. Did you get burned at all?"

"No. Just my arms. It's not a big deal, Mom." I pointed at the house we stopped in front of. "Do you think we could stay here tonight?"

Pressing her lips together, Mom cast a fleeting look over her shoulder and then back to me. "No, I'm sorry. I know you're tired and ready to stop for the night, but we need to keep going. We're supposed to be at the checkpoint in two days. At this rate, we might not make it in a week." She slowly caught her breath as she focused on inhaling through her nose and exhaling through rounded lips.

Her priorities had shifted from working and crafts to center around the checkpoint, the camp, the group, the preparations, etc. Nothing ever came before preparing for the impending war. Even her prayer circle had its own time and place. Mom only went to church if she determined the situation was safe. Too many people trying to topple Christ, she said.

I didn't know anything about that. All I knew was that most of the kids at school had left to be homeschooled and the ones who continued attending were too scared to ask their parents if the world was crashing while we sat unprotected at our desks.

In my case, I guess I should've asked about being unprotected in the bathroom. Oh, crap What if I had actually been using the toilet when the bombs had started? A shiver trickled through me, standing my arm hair on end.

"Kelly, are you listening to me?" Mom snapped her fingers in front of my eyes. Her nails were cut short and she'd been picking at her cuticles.

I blinked. "Yes, I am. What are we going to do?"

"We're going to go over the rules again while we take another second to catch our breath. After, we'll find a place to make camp. We can go down early, so we can get an early start." She lifted three fingers. "Name—"

Cutting her off, I covered her hand with mine. How did I make her understand I wasn't a toddler? "I know the rules, Mom. You don't have to keep reciting them to me."

"Then let's hear them. In the proper order, Kelly." She arched her eyebrows and waited, not lowering her hand.

The proper order. Always the order. If she didn't stop issuing demands, I would consider changing the *order*, just to set her on edge. Okay, it was a weak threat, but I was too tired and irritated to play her games. Yes, thankfully, she had been prepared for the chaos, but part of me worried maybe everything had happened because of people like Mom who had worried it into happening.

Oh, wow, I better play along before my fatigue had me convinced Mom was the one behind the entire world falling apart.

Clenching my teeth, I inhaled through my nose. To give her the benefit of the doubt, I could believe she didn't know how irritating the repetition was. She might not know her rules didn't fit with what I was trying to do with my life. But the resolve in her set jaw and tightening of her cheeks indicated none of that mattered.

I glanced at her hand, the fingers waiting for me with more patience than her expression. Fighting the urge to roll my eyes, I muttered. "Pray. Trust no one. Stay alive." While staying alive fit in with my plans, I couldn't guarantee that I wouldn't trust people, and praying just wasn't me.

Her faith hadn't passed to me like her brunette hair and blue eyes had. Faith had skipped me as surely as Bodey, the captain of the math team – yep, homeschooled, too – had passed me by. Over and over. Like I didn't exist. Since he'd graduated my opportunities had become more scarce to try for his attention. Even though we knew each other and often said hi, he wouldn't think about me right then... not at the end of the world.

Didn't matter now. He was probably dead. Like everyone else.

She inclined her head, finally dropping her hand. "Good. Let's get to the forest, break to the north of Rathdrum, and stop. We should be out of the immediate crowds and a closer to the checkpoint."

What crowds? I nodded. Even frustrated I wouldn't abandon her. No way would I leave Mom, not when we only had each other. Where would I go? Running away wasn't my style, especially at the beginning of a war predicted by historians as the war to obliterate the human species. People interested in history could be so vague.

Plus, she was all I had. I couldn't forget that.

And I loved her. My mom.

We fell into step again, me behind, like a practiced funeral march.

~~~

Left, right, left, right, left, right. Oh, for the love, I almost fell over on that one. I shook my head to wake up. We had been walking for quite a while. An hour or two?

The darkness of night had fallen to mask the majority of the scenery around us. There was no light anywhere – except in the sky.

"I've never seen so many stars." My mom's whisper reached me as I walked forward, coming abreast of her.

Glancing upward, even in my fatigue I couldn't deny the simple beauty laid out over me like the thickest of blankets with no end in sight. "Yeah, me neither."

"Do you know God intended for His children to outnumber the stars?" Mom didn't slow her steps, but spoke into the black void around us, with her head tilted back to view the skies.

I didn't answer. Everything she said would turn back to her beliefs. When Dad and Braden hadn't come back home, I had looked away from the faith she held so close. What guiding hand would take a father and son who hadn't done anything? During school at the time, I think we had been studying something from the *Naturalist's Handbook*. The theories in those pages had been easier to grasp than the one which stated I "was loved and redeemed but my family didn't get to stay."

Nothing seemed fair since.

Changing the subject, I pointed at the houses in the distance – their rooftops stark against the well-lit night sky. "Looks like the electricity is out everywhere. Do you think anybody *wasn't* affected?"

"If not, it wouldn't be for long. We're too close to the Fairchild Air Force Base. Of course, our area would take the brunt of the attack. If we head too far east, we'll run into the missile fields of Montana and the Navy bases of Athol and Sandpoint. Straight north of Post Falls? We're looking at a richer option – one filled with others who think like us as well as a small community for the safer-group co-op – just north of here." She didn't even hunch over as she walked with the weight of her bag on her shoulders.

"Can we use our flashlights?" My logic made sense. With no one around to see the light, we didn't have anything to be in danger of. We could walk with a faster pace if we didn't need to squint at anything we weren't ready for. "Nobody's out here."

"No, using them just wouldn't be smart. Noises are already stupid, but add in lights? We might as well hold up a neon sign to our location. People are out there. Trust me." She veered off the sidewalk and walked through someone's yard.

Suddenly we left the illusion of a safe fenced-in-mentality of a neighborhood and entered the forest. Hopefully, we would lose ourselves in the dark twists and turns as we located somewhere to camp.

I refused to argue. We'd left the monotony of the sidewalks and landed on a smoothly packed gravel drive. At least the crunch of my footsteps created enough distraction I didn't fall asleep with the cadence.

Another thirty minutes or so passed in silence.

Mom stopped abruptly and I slammed into her back. "Oh, sorry."

"Shh." She shook her head and grabbed my arm. Pointing off the drive, she muttered. "We'll make camp in there. Remember the rules, Kelly, and you'll be fine." She leaned over and squeezed me. I'm not sure what she was getting at with the pseudo-comfort, but her reassurances were there and I'm not too proud to admit it worked.

CHAPTER 4

The direction Mom pointed took us over a roughed-in trail with low hanging branches. Walking another five minutes at a sketchy pace I hesitated to actually call a walk, we stopped in a clearing about ten feet wide – just enough to let the starlight in.

We set up our sleeping rolls at the base of a tree whose shadow suggested it was gnarled and twisted, entwined with another trunk. Soft deadfall from the previous autumn and winter muffled our movements as we shuffled around our temporary site.

Spring in the northwest is notorious for warm days and chilly nights. The temperature had dropped with the setting of the sun hours before and I shivered in my multiple layers.

Mom reached into my backpack's extra side pocket – the thing had a ton of those – and pulled out a balaclava which she tossed at me. "Pull this on. You'll be warmer sleeping in it."

I pulled the full-headed hat over my tight bun. The mask part covered my mouth and nose. Fleece always gave an illusion of instant warmth. I didn't want to focus on the warm memories of Braden and I laughing at the name the first time we'd heard it. Balaclava sounded like baklava the amazing Turkish pastry Dad loved so much. Braden had tried licking my head the entire day I'd had that stupid hat on, he kept saying how yummy my head looked.

Little Braden. Loved that kid.

Missed that kid.

Tears pricked at my eyes and my mouth dried up. Braden would be twelve, if he were still alive. Five years younger than me. He would nudge me as we ate something Mom gave us and giggling. Braden always giggled.

Dad would turn to us and lift his eyebrow, while holding Mom's hand. He always touched her, hand-holding or twirling a piece of her hair, or brushing his fingers over her shoulder. Dad had loved Mom even without telling her.

Breaking through my reverie, Mom's abrupt movements didn't rough up the silence of the hour. "Don't unpack too much. We're only sleeping here, and not for long. Not even the full night, okay?" Her voice barely carried to me as she hunkered down on the ground in a half-squat with her sleeping bag wrapped around her shoulders and back.

She dug into one of her bag's pockets, tossing me a dense protein bar, a banana, and another sandwich. "Eat that. They'll stick with you a while longer than a normal candy bar."

I didn't question her logic as I tore open the plastic wrapper and bit off a chunk. The rustling of the cellophane startled me with its loudness, but didn't stop me. Mom could have given me a plate of weeds and rocks and I could have eaten it without argument. "Thanks, Mom." I mumbled around the thick grainy snack.

Braden had hated those stupid bars.

She folded her hands and closed her eyes, bowing her head.

Lately, I ignored prayers at dinner and at bedtime. My mom, she never forgot. I shifted uncomfortably on the leaves beneath my butt and chewed slower until she lifted her head and took her first bite. Like, if I paused or something it would be enough reverence for whomever she spoke to.

She swallowed, the movement barely recognizable in the dark. "Don't drink too much water, you don't want to need to use the bathroom out here this late at night." I know survival was the name of the game, but she could've relaxed a bit, at least try not to sound like a demanding drill sergeant all the time.

We finished eating in silence. She held out her hand and I passed her my garbage before sipping – only sipping – from my water bottle. Pushing our backpacks against the tree, she motioned for me to turn around. I spun on my rear and we lay down, back to back.

Security from having my mom so close to me stabilized my nerves. My breathing deepened. With a soft breeze tickling the leaves and needles overhead, I drifted easily into a solid sleep.

~~~

I rubbed my nose, blinking into the blacker night – blacker? How was that even possible? But my breath rebounded into my face. The balaclava had slipped up over my face, covering my eyes as well.

A small tug pulled the hood back into position. The night *had* deepened. Stars blinked brighter like I could reach up and push them around. What had wakened me?

Thud. Angry male voices carried on the muted night air.

A person cried out. Like a woman. Like —

I reached out behind me, sitting up, grasping for Mom in the tousled pile of sleeping bag and needles.

My hand only crinkled the empty blanket. Turning fully around, I slapped the blanket in case she had fallen asleep and I hadn't woken her up. The blanket sank beneath my hits and I encountered nothing but sleeping bag.

Unable to fully comprehend what was happening, I gripped the edges of her bag and shoved it fully into the top of her pack. Once I loaded it all the way, I zipped the pocket closed and did the same with my bag and pack.

Seconds. I didn't have more than seconds. In all the practices Mom had me run through, she hammered the importance of time into my head.

I didn't dare speak or make a sound. She had taught me on our camping trips that in survival situations, more times than not, men sought a way to hurt women and women would find a way to survive – even if that meant stealing or killing.

Her knowledge had never seemed more real than in that dark moment on the ground. Mom had purchased bags we could strap onto each other in case either of us needed to carry more than one bag. Connecting them, I reached into the hidden pocket on the back of Mom's bag and pulled out her .9 mm Glock. The gun's commanding size weighed down my wrists.

Firing the thing had become second nature to both my mom and me. Multiple weekends camping and shooting in the woods would do that to a girl and her mom. Especially after Dad and Braden hadn't returned from their trip.

I drew the double-pack on my back, tucking my chin at the excess weight.

Hide. I had to hide.

Large bushes lined the west part of the clearing Mom had brought us to. I bear-crawled to the low hanging branches and tucked in underneath. Bugs and spiders and all kinds of creepy things most likely called that place home, but I bit my inner cheek and stared out into the night.

Gripping the handle of the gun, I held the weapon on the ground by my face. Cold metal reminded me I couldn't cry or make a sound. I had a dang gun beside my cheek!

The only thing keeping me from chasing after Mom was her orders to not look for her, if anything happened. But oh, my gosh, I couldn't... what if? Too many variables – too many to contemplate and NOT chase after her. Find her.

But she'd ordered me to never chase after her because it could be endangering to both of us.

I didn't want her in more danger.

Mom had to make it back. What was happening to her? For the first time in a long while, I closed my eyes and whispered to anyone who might be listening. "Please, bring her back. Please."

~~~

The snapping of a twig off to my right woke me from what had to be the worst night of sleep I'd ever had. Rubbing my eyes, I winced at the sensation of sand under my eyelids from exhaustion.

Dawn crept in, pinks and oranges mixing softly with whites and creams. As hard as I tried, I couldn't hear my mom the rest of the night.

I shifted my head from the side of the gun I had ended up using as a makeshift pillow.

Where had Mom gone? Why wasn't she by me and why hadn't the men gotten me too?

Another sound, like the scuffing of a heavy boot on rocks drew my attention to the right of my hiding place. I crept backward a few more inches. The bush might not be large enough to cover me. What if my feet hung out the other side?

My fingers hurt from holding the firearm so long. I switched to the other hand, my fingers tight and crooked, almost numb.

A cough and more dragging and footfalls held my stare like a crash site. I couldn't look away from the approximate spot the noise came from.

Something crawled along the back of my hand. I swallowed my shriek and brushed it off without passing out. Bugs. I hated bugs. Oh, man, how I hated them. A shiver skimmed down my neck. *Yes, a shiver, a shiver, a shiver. Please not another bug. Please. Oh, please.*

Braden used to throw fake ones over the curtains while I stood in the shower. Wow, that was just two years ago. A wave of sadness engulfed me as I struggled to stay calm.

Then, as if magically conjured, two men appeared on the edge of the clearing. Between them they dragged what I could only assume was Mom. *My* mom. And she wasn't conscious. Her head bobbed with each step and they dragged her over the uneven ground. Each had a hold of an arm.

I bit my lip, intent on them not seeing me, like my own will determined what people saw or didn't see. Was she still alive?

The man closest to me stopped short and kicked at the ground. "Are you sure she came from this way?" His deep low tones could've been on a radio.

"Look, man, I know what I saw. She can't be alone. If she is? She won't be without supplies. She's gotta be worth something, either way." The second man tugged on Mom's arm like a tow-strap. "Come on. She's not light."

I held my breath as they passed five feet from me. From my angle, Mom's discolored face tore through me. His last line – she's not light – filled me with rage. Like my mom was a bag or animal or something. She could be annoying, but she wasn't heavy for crying out loud. She was my mom!

Clenching the butt of the gun until my knuckles cracked, I closed my eyes when they left my view. What was I going to do? I couldn't leave her with them. She needed me. Was I going to sit there and wait for more bugs to crawl on me?

One, two, three… I found the pace of my pulse and counted… eight, nine, ten. A trick I learned running. Find my pulse or my footsteps and keep time. Let the numbers do their thing. Thirty-nine, forty, forty-one.

When I reached one-hundred, I Army-crawled from beneath the bushes and leaves. Standing, I brushed at every inch of my head, back, chest, legs, and arms I could reach.

Everything got a shake down. Nothing was going to harbor any bugs. I'd read about ticks and other things. I shuddered, pulling my shoulders back and thrusting my chin forward.

The balaclava had helped me keep the majority of them out of my hair. For a while anyway, that thing wasn't coming off.

With a jostle to position the packs higher on my back, I headed off in the direction the men had disappeared. Gripping the gun, I couldn't help the small tic of my pointer finger tapping the trigger guard. Muzzle down, I wouldn't hit anything important, but the movement made me confident since I had a gun so handy.

Oh, but even if I was really great – like the greatest shot ever – I would still only hit like twenty-five percent of my targets. Even at the gun range, I only ever hit five percent. Five percent! I didn't stand a chance. Especially if the men moved.

Uncertainty faltered my footsteps and I stumbled like an actual object had jumped out and tripped me.

Grabbing the nearest tree trunk, I leaned against the rough bark for a brief moment. What was I doing? *Come on, Kelly. Come on.* Mom knew this could happen. We prepared for everything. Even how to survive alone, if we had to.

Mom hadn't covered how to track on our campouts, though, and that particular skill wasn't exactly something the school district had included in their curriculum.

I fiddled with the paracord bracelet my mom made me wear all the time. Fitted with a magnifying glass and compass, the intricate braiding wended over a half-razor blade and a needle. My survival jewelry. Wasn't I cool? Fat lot of good it did me.

Hopefully I wouldn't get close enough to the men I would be able to use a dang razor.

A fine sweat beaded my forehead. Not enough to make me remove the balaclava. No way.

Somehow their voices had faded. What if I had lost them while holding that dang tree up?

I stepped forward, hands reaching for the straps at my shoulders. I had to make up some ground. Ten feet, fifteen feet passed, I stared at the grass and dark, wet leaves as I placed my boots one in front of the other. If I kept the fear at bay, I would be able to find her and help. If I gave in, I would sit down and cry like a dang baby and lose her for good.

Why couldn't I hear them?

Right then, one of the men laughed, like a braying donkey and I jerked backwards beside a new tree. Ducking behind the branches, I peered toward the direction of the noise and breathed deep with relief? Or fear, but I wouldn't admit that to anyone.

I had almost walked in on them.

Their clearing opened up abruptly from the thick forest. Tarps hung from ropes strung between trees. Attempts at a fire cluttered under an over-stacked fire pyramid even I could see wouldn't start a smoke-out let alone a fire.

Red coolers stacked beside a five gallon water dispenser set up on a larger gray cooler.

The guys dropped Mom beside a tree, thankfully one closer to me and not on the other side of the larger clearing. They attacked the top cooler like a pack of ravenous wolves. Both emerged with a six-pack of canned beer.

Whooping and hollering, they skipped to two trunk-sized logs set on their ends around the makeshift fire pit.

I allowed myself to take inventory of as much of Mom as I could from my vantage point. She didn't stir. Dirt smudged her forehead and nose. Her features had never seemed so delicate. She couldn't help me or tell me what to do. She wasn't moving. What if I couldn't wake her up? I couldn't drag her out of there on my own. Not with our bags.

What was I going to do? Hopelessness created a hole inside me. What was I supposed to do?

Focus. Just focus. What did I need to do? First of all, I wouldn't be able to *do* anything with both packs weighing me down. My lower back ached in protest at the thought.

Keeping my eye on the two men as they repeatedly raised cans to their mouths, I slowly slid the bags from my shoulders. I softly settled them under the branches of the tree I hid behind and straightened my back to stretch the tightness out.

Mom's absolute stillness worried me. Even if I did get in there, how would I get her out while holding a gun on the men? This wasn't the movies and I wasn't a cop or anything spectacular. I was just me. What could I do?

Not much standing by the bags doing nothing.

I stood straighter with less weight and stretched my neck side to side. I could channel one of my favorite action stars and be like all tough or something. My inner cheek succumbed to my nervous nibbles and I inhaled shakily.

Okay, I could pretend to be something *other* than me. With my heart racing, I would try anything.

Both men tossed empty cans over their shoulders. I jumped as the aluminum hitting the ground tinged in the still air. Another beer in each man's hands and they chugged those down, too.

While I'm standing there, nervous as all get out, they're drinking. Drinking!

Come on, really? As soon as the second cans join the first round, the third can was opened and draining. Like a race. Maybe the alcohol would hit them soon and they would fall asleep or something.

But one stands up, third beer in hand, and heads toward my mom. "Hey, Shane, let's have some fun with this one."

Fun? I wasn't naïve. Men didn't have any other concept of fun besides sex. I'd just never done it myself. Watching two men rape my mother wasn't on my list of things to do before I died. Or she died.

Crap, no one was dying!

Before I could talk myself out of anything stupid or rash, I stepped out from behind the tree and aimed the gun at the men. I forced confidence into my voice and yelled. "Stop. Don't touch her."

They turned. Shane was slower to react. He couldn't focus on me or anything, and his partner narrowed his eyes. "Well, well, well, a little one. Come on, little one. We'll take you first. See what's behind that mask." He revealed teeth lined in gray. He stepped toward me, his lips drawn back in something I think he meant to pass off as a smile, but came off looking feral.

He tilted his head back and finished his drink, tossing the can to the side. He fumbled with his belt, eyes never straying from a direct line on me. His fingers moved to his zipper and button.

Disgusted, I glanced toward Shane.

The man with the undone pants took another step but I refused to back up.

Shane lurched toward my mom. He tottered above her but found his balance enough to draw back his foot and kick her in the ribs. For his sake, he better be drunk enough to not have much power in his efforts.

At the same time, the first jerk stepped again toward me.

I reached my final straw. My finger slid into place and I pulled, hard, more than ready for the kickback from the strong gun.

The shot firing resonated around the clearing, rebounding into the forest off a tree and another tree and another like a pinball machine.

Oh wow, had I just shot someone?

B. R. PAULSON

CHAPTER 5

Oh my word, oh my word, oh my word.

Blood dripped from the fallen man's upper thigh. The copper scent warred with suddenly overwhelming pine. My senses heightened and I swear a fly buzzed somewhere off to my right.

I didn't lower the gun because Shane didn't move to help his friend. He stared with his mouth hanging open at the wound. His eyes flicked my direction then back to the guy crying on the ground.

Making men cry wasn't on my daily to-do list, but it felt good in that instance. Jerks.

Gritting my teeth, I willed everything I had into stopping my hands from shaking.

Seriously, stop, already. If I showed any weakness, he could tackle me. At least, I could picture him doing it. He hadn't actually moved much since the beers and with the lack of focus in his expression, I couldn't be sure he wasn't partially harmless.

While the civilized part of me longed to say I'm sorry, I'm sorry, to the guy I shot, I couldn't bring myself to move my mouth. Because I wasn't. Not even enough that my civilized side could still be referred to as civilized. I wanted to be sorry. Wanted to be a good person who didn't want to shoot people and who wanted to pray and have faith like my mom. I guarantee she would have forgiven them and not had to shoot anyone.

In fact, if honesty were my claim to greatness, I would say a bigger, meaner part of me wanted to shoot Shane twice as much as the other guy out of revenge for hurting Mom.

If that made me a bad person, I didn't want to be a good one.

Mom moaned, drawing my attention and Shane's. She turned her head back and forth on the ground, pieces of leaves and blades of grass clung to the waves of her still-mostly dark hair. Lashes fluttering, she stilled. Had she woken up? Was she aware or had she slipped away again?

Shane ignored me. He stepped toward her, outstretching his hands like he'd forgotten all about me. His swaying stopped but he had an unclear haze to his expression, like he couldn't focus. When he bent over, arms still out, it didn't matter if he was inebriated or not. I didn't care about him and he became less human the closer he got to Mom.

Before he could touch her, I commanded in a low firm voice. "Don't get any closer. I'll shoot you." And by all that was holy I would. My hands steadied and I aimed easily at his chest.

Heck, I already shot one guy – okay, it was an accident – but the act hadn't been as bad as I expected. I might need to try again to see if it was a one-time thing or actually got easier with each one.

He froze, glancing over his shoulder to his friend still moaning and compressing his leg with tight fingers. Shane glared at me, narrowing his eyes. A weasely nose and narrowed jaw-line didn't give me any reassurances he would stay put once we left. I had to tie him up.

Tears pricked the backs of my eyes. I wouldn't cry in front of them. I could control that much, but I just shot someone and my mom was in danger and I had no idea what I was doing.

Mom opened her eyes and stared at the man above her for one, two, thre—

She scrambled to her feet and backed up, taking in as much of the scene as she could in only a matter of heart beats. Once she perused everything around her, she side-stepped toward me, hand outstretched.

I tried ignoring the blood leaking from her nose and the horrific purple and blue bruising already coloring around her temple and upper cheekbone. In disarray, her hair only made her look more wild. My all-powerful mom had vulnerabilities and right then wasn't the time to spot them.

When she got within reach, I gratefully handed the gun to her, keeping my eyes on the men in case they chose to try something. Nausea wrangled with my stomach and if I didn't get out of there soon, I had a sinking sensation it was going to win.

"Back up, beside the other one." One-handed, Mom motioned toward the downed would-be-abductor with the muzzle of the gun. With her other arm, she corralled me behind her and backed us out.

Shane moved slowly as if he couldn't quite grasp what was happening. He stopped beside the guy who hadn't stopped crying. The sound of a man crying in pain was more annoying than anything.

I'd never heard my dad cry, never thought of him as a crier and it hadn't occurred to me that he might have lost some tears at the end.

"Shane, I think she hit my crotch, man." The guy rocked back and forth with his hand pushed tight against his upper leg.

For the record, the outside of his leg is nowhere near his crotch.

I sighed, suddenly not so nauseated.

Shane didn't take his eyes off us. Even glassy, his gaze didn't flicker. So he couldn't be too drunk. Seniors used to come like that to class. Idiots.

"If we see you again, we'll shoot you where it counts." Mom tilted her head, steady. "I don't miss, either." Under her breath, she muttered. "Go get their guns over by the tree. The two rifles. We might be able to use them. Hurry, we need to get going."

First, I back up and grabbed the doubled-up backpacks and drew them onto my shoulders.

The tree supporting the weapons was past the men but I skirted the rounded edge of the clearing and reached it without going within arm's reach of them.

With both backpacks on, grabbing the heavy guns wasn't easy. But I lifted them and carried one leaning over each shoulder without complaint. Mom couldn't carry them. At least not yet and I wasn't going to take her for granted again – at least not in the immediate future.

In that moment, I'd gladly do whatever it took to get somewhere safe. With my mom.

The coppery scent of blood rode the morning breeze and I wrinkled my nose. A biology fact rose to the surface of my memory about sharks in the ocean. Something about smelling a drop of blood from a mile away. I couldn't remember if they had a predator with those capabilities in the northwestern forests. If we did, well, Shane and his buddy weren't going to do very well.

I reached my mom. Resolving to keep my mouth shut and not argue, I backed up until I was behind Mom again and followed her lead as we backed out of the clearing.

If the men survived, I had a sinking sensation, we would see them again. They would no longer be the prey lying like bait for any predator to come along. Instead, they would be like sharks and their revenge wouldn't be glorious or natural.

That didn't make tomorrow look any brighter.

CHAPTER 6

Small puffy clouds teased me by not moving in the sky as we walked down the same gravel road. I couldn't find anything to help me figure out how much time had passed. Watches weren't my thing, never had been, and I wasn't the type of person that could make a time piece with a pine needle and acorn shell. If that was such a thing.

Another foot in front of the other. Another. Another. How many was that? I lost count what seemed like years ago. Somehow the effort to just breathe had increased since I shot that man.

Guilt weighed on me. Not because I shot him, but because I most likely had given a reason to someone to chase after us. I used to read books about that type of thing – before the government had shut down libraries.

We passed under some shade from a collection of gathered aspens.

I froze. I couldn't take another step. Not one more. Bending at the waist, I braced my hands on my lower thighs and locked my knees. "Mom." I gasped. Despair welled inside me. My tongue hurt and my eyes burned.

Why couldn't I breathe?

Her feet scuffed over the gravel as she turned and picked up the pace, closing the distance between us. When had she gotten so far away? I hadn't noticed.

She reached me, resting her hand on my shoulder and bending to meet me at my level. "Kelly, are you okay?" Mom forced me to release my hold on my knees and half-straightened me to remove my backpack. She'd taken hers off and placed them along with the rifles against the side of a small ditch.

Shrugging from her own burdens, she set mine on the ground and pushed me to stand. "Lift your arms. Look up. Good. You're okay, breathe in and out. Nice and even. Are you okay?" When my mom had worked full time as a nurse, I always wondered if she really knew her stuff.

Even when we rarely saw a doctor because she always tended to us, I still doubted her.

Looking up didn't help. My lips wanted to part but I fought to hold them together. Moisture – no, I couldn't admit to tears, not yet, not again – filled my eyes and I dragged in a ragged gasp. The air refused to rest in me and pushed back out on a long painful sob.

Mom wrapped her arm around my shoulders and pulled me in for a tight hug. She glanced around, leading me toward a clear spot inside the tree line. Grabbing our bags and the guns, she returned to sit beside me.

The cover of the branches somehow released the tight imaginary band constricting my chest.

I cried, unable to define why. Pinpointing the exact reason didn't seem as important as getting the pain out.

With a quick jerk, I turned into my mom's arms and pressed my cheek to her shoulder. I gripped her with both hands.

And I cried. I sobbed.

The tears wouldn't stop, but the relief grew. Things didn't feel wound so tight.

Mom stroked my head under the damp balaclava. The morning hadn't passed fast enough that it was too warm to wear the covering. "Shh. I know. It's okay to cry. Let's eat while we're here.

How does that sound? We're both tired." She patted my back as my erratic sobbing subsided and I sniffed.

Food? Of course that sounded alright. Her hands moved gracefully between our bags as she pulled out individually wrapped sandwiches and pickles in baggies. With a sheepish grin, Mom passed me a turkey sandwich. "We can start eating other stuff after the sandwiches are gone."

She bowed her head and silently blessed her meal. I avoided her eyes when she lifted her gaze. Motioning with her sandwich toward the road, she raised her eyebrows. "What was with all the crying? Did you hurt yourself?"

I shook my head. The last thing I wanted was to sound like a coward, but I needed someone else to hear the insanity in my head. "I didn't mean to shoot anyone. I wanted to fire a warning shot into the ground by his feet."

Mom lowered her sandwich and slowly chewed the bite in her mouth. She swallowed, watching me. "What do you mean? You shot him pretty clean. You know how to shoot."

Heat flooded my face over my behavior. I shifted on the lumpy ground. Cool moisture dampened the backs of my thighs and I crossed my legs Indian style. "Well..." I stared at the sandwich resting on my leg. Did I tell her I was petrified? Not for any solid reason, but more like I feared karma – something she never believed in.

Another thing about me and Mom that didn't fit – I worried about things being true whether I believed in them or not. She had complete faith what she believed was end-all-be-all. Therefore, karma didn't concern her.

If karma had been a true belief of mine, I would be comfortable knowing I'd shot that guy. Those men had been about to do something even more horrible than kidnapping and beating my mom and karma had come along and taken my accidental shot and shoved the bullet into a leg.

If I believed karma had a role, I couldn't say I would feel too bad at that point.

I shrugged. "No, like I said, I aimed for the ground. I didn't want to hurt anyone, only scare them, you know? Make them think I meant it?" In the movies actions like that always went well. Why couldn't mine work?

Mom chuckled and bit into her sandwich again. I raised mine, hungry and yet still nervous all at once.

"Your first shot on a living thing is what's bothering you. Plus, you're so much like your dad. Let me guess, you're wondering if that guy had deserved to be shot, right? Or maybe now that you did what you did, what's going to happen to you?" She watched me, waiting for my answer.

I nodded, hunkering my shoulders in shame I didn't want to feel. "I wanted to save you, but I was hoping to do it without hurting anyone." Plus, what if they ignored Mom's warning and they came after us? Two men against two petite-sized women? We would be screwed.

"Well, you did save me. I'm going to rely on the Old Testament's teachings right now and hold to the practice of an eye-for-an-eye." She paused, looking down at her sandwich and inhaling heavily. Lowering her sandwich to her lap, her gaze met mine. "Okay, I'm sorry. That's not what I meant. I don't want to exact revenge on anyone. I..." she picked at the seam of her pants, pinching and rolling the small amount of excess material. "You're not ready to be on your own yet. Those men are nothing compared to what I can only imagine is out there for us to face." She shook her head. "You're not ready."

"Mom, I'm stronger than you think. I promise I can handle more. You don't need to worry about me." How did I tell her I'd already been kissed? Kids at school teased me about still having my V-card, but that wasn't anyone's business. I wasn't rolling over for just anyone. And the boys at my school were *just anyone*. Unless of course you count Bodey Christianson. Seriously, the boy was smart as heck and hot, too.

But I didn't count him because he didn't go to my school technically. Did he count, if he was dead?

"Why did you leave your sleeping bag? How did those guys get you?" I played with the plastic corner of my baggie. I hadn't asked yet because the full import of how much danger we'd been in hadn't disappeared from my nerves.

Mom blushed. "I had to use the bathroom. I told *you* not to drink too much water and I almost emptied my canteen. I walked a little ways away so I wouldn't wake you and wasn't paying attention. Didn't even take my gun." She shook her head. "All that preaching about camp rules and safety and I'd abandoned every single one of them."

Now that we were safe, I chuckled, but shakily. "That's not funny, but it is. Sounds more like something I would do."

"Nah, Kelly. Give yourself more credit. We're all human. We all make mistakes. I'm glad you were brave enough to fix mine." She leaned over and shoulder-squeezed me in a half-hug.

We ate together in silence, Mom thoughtful as she finished her pickle and sipped water.

Nothing about the sandwich was spectacular. I mean, seriously, what was dramatic about mayonnaise, mustard, cheese, and deli-turkey meat? Not a lot. But since I hadn't eaten in a while and after the exhausting ordeal with the men, the sandwich and pickle could've been from a five-star restaurant in Seattle.

The full sensation hit me after a few minutes and I moaned.

So glad to not be hungry, I ignored the worry a simple thought brought to the forefront – I had only gone eight hours or so without food. Things were guaranteed to get worse.

Could I survive without comfort and convenience? Or had my mom's training weekends and week-to-month-long training sessions been in vain?

Mom collected my baggies and tucked them into another small pocket on her backpack.

Glancing behind us, I blinked at the ever-clearing sky. "Hey, the smoke has stopped. Maybe we can go back?"

"No smoke isn't reassuring, Kelly. If the bombing stopped, whoever attacked got what they wanted." She fell silent, arranging her pack on her shoulders. Matter-of-factly, she helped load mine on my back and patted the bottom of the bag before walking around me. "We're almost to the turnout. Let's keep going." She glanced at my face then over my shoulder. "Stop looking back. We'll never see our world the way it was."

Tears built in my eyes again, but Mom's? They were clear as if she'd just woken up from a restful night.

An hour later a pinching burn on the pinky side of my foot got my attention. I walked on the inside of my foot, trying to take the weight off that side, but the pain only abated for a few steps before returning with a heated anger.

So I limped, but the change in stride didn't work either. Shuffling to the side of the road, I leaned my shoulder against a tree. "Mom." I didn't speak too loud. We didn't need a repeat of last night and that morning.

A lot of noise wasn't necessary. Concern knitting her eyebrows together, she backtracked to me. She studied the scenery, then pressed her face close to mine. "What's wrong?"

"My foot is killing me." I whispered, trying not to groan.

"Did you double up your socks?" She knelt, untying my hiking boot with fast hard motions.

I glared at the tree limbs overhead. Of course not. Why would I remember something she'd told me to do a hundred times before the world crashed down around us? Because I was an idiot. Blisters could be avoided. Heat flooded my face and I shook my head enough to move my hair but not enough to further my embarrassment.

Mom sighed. "Come on, Kelly. You have to do the basics."

"I know." I kept my voice tight. No reason to add to her "told you so" moment.

"Hey, don't get lippy with me. If you know how to avoid this, then it's on your shoulders." She slid my shoe off and then my sock, careful on the tender side of my foot. Her gentleness irritated me. When I was being rude, she should be rude back. It was only polite.

"Yes, Mom." My extra socks were in the bottom of my backpack. Hopefully she didn't ask me for them. I could handle only so much humility and with a blister burning my foot, right then wasn't the time to add more.

She pulled a bandaid from her jacket pocket and stuck it to my foot over the reddish area. Whipping my sock back on and then my shoe, she tied the laces before standing. "That'll work until we get an extra sock out of the bag."

"Thanks, Mom." I grumbled, irritated I had to be grateful about anything. I gingerly stepped on the foot. A little bit of soreness persisted but nothing like before.

"Sure. You're just tired. Come on, up ahead at the next bend we'll go into the woods. I'm not sure what the trails will be like right now, so we have to be cautious." She wiped her hands on her thighs, watching the road in front of us.

"We haven't seen anyone else this way, which is weird for such a large number in our co-op." She didn't look confused, instead worry added a downturned slant to her lips. "We'll keep praying for help."

"Yeah, okay." I fell into step beside her, my head pounding from the lack of solid sleep. As irritated as I got with Mom, I had to give it to her. She was a monster with her discipline. She would probably tack her strength up to faith or something, but I dialed it in as craziness. Still her *craziness* was keeping us alive.

Shafts of sunlight enhanced the brilliant green trees and the grasses freshly sprouting from damp earth. We climbed the ditch from the gravel to the sloping forest floor.

The pain had dramatically decreased in my foot and even fatigued, I couldn't hold back my optimism. Hopefully, where we were going had good food and a shelter. Maybe I could wash my hair, or better yet, take a shower. I needed to pee on a toilet – bad. The excitement of using bushes for cover had died long ago.

We climbed about fifty feet. In front of us, laid out like a viewing at a funeral, a fallen tree whose circumference I would never be able to wrap my arms around waited in rest like Sleeping Beauty. Green moss and lichen decorated the creases and grooves. Flower buds sprouted from the mosses and poked from the deepest green centers of the collections. I couldn't help myself and ran my fingers over the velvety coverings.

Mom paused, looking behind us. She kneeled and motioned I follow.

Knees in the dirt, she pointed past the end of the log toward a dense copse of trees. Whispering lower than before, she barely moved her lips. "I don't know who or what we're going to find. It's way too quiet. You do exactly what I say. Keep the balaclava on. I don't care how hot you get, do you understand?"

I nodded, leery of arguing in case she was right. The balaclava wasn't uncomfortable so agreeing didn't hurt me any.

Together we rose and stepped cautiously around the tree. The ground covering absorbed our footprints and as I looked back, they disappeared as if we'd never been there.

We entered the thicker tree line and Mom grabbed my arm. She pushed me behind a tree and shook her head. Pointing toward a suddenly-present clearing, she mouthed. "Looks like a fight."

She'd gauged the assumption fast. I poked my head around the rough trunk, scratching my cheek in the process. Rubbing the offended part, I stared at the scattered garbage and broken glass littering the well-packed dirt clearing. Smaller fallen logs, set up like seating around a fire pit, framed spread dead coals around the grass. A torn down tent fluttered in the soft breeze, poles poking into the air like a beetle on its back.

Mom motioned me back.

I moved to retreat, but stopped when she lowered her flattened fingers to the ground in a swift jerking move. Returning to my spot, I peered back to the clearing. A different shade of green from the surrounding forest moved slightly on the far border of the clearing.

A woman stared back at us. Her long dark blonde hair lay in a thick braid over her shoulder. Tight jeans and an even tighter sweater suggested she came into the end with something else on her mind than practicality.

She reached for something at her waist.

Mom tensed, reaching for her waist as well.

What did I do? Witnessing a shootout wasn't my idea of surviving anything.

Was the woman as good a shot as my mom?

CHAPTER 7

"Megan, is that you?" The woman ducked her head as she peered toward my mom.

My gaze volleyed between them. I held my breath. Did Mom know her? Or was she like the men we escaped from?

Hand still at the ready, Mom called back. "Jeanine? Where is everyone?"

"Let me come over." Instead of running across the litter strewn clearing like I expected, Jeanine dodged around the edge, disappearing behind trees and bushes as she walked.

Stashing the rifles behind a split tree off the main path, Mom pushed me further from the open clearing. She grabbed my hand and glared hard into my eyes. She obviously didn't want me to talk, but could she have also wanted me to stop breathing?

Hard telling when she assumed I could read her mind.

Surprisingly quiet, Jeanine reached us in less than a minute. She flipped her long braid behind her shoulder as she perused the woods around us. She leaned forward and air hugged Mom, ignoring me for the moment. "I'm not sure how far our voices carry out here." She murmured.

Mom pulled me closer to her side. "What happened?"

Jeanine heaved a sigh. "Charlie and Shane never showed up. They were supposed to be our south periphery protection. Without them here and, Larry didn't show up either, well, things fell apart. Ryan and Joseph fought for control. We went up to Larry's since he has the best set up and to check on him. Everyone who showed up went that way."

We'd just met someone named Shane, could it be coincidence?

"How many?" Mom's fingers clenched on my forearm, like nerves controlled her hands and spasmed.

Grimacing to the side, Jeanine bowed her head. "Only about half. We can function with only four, if we need to."

Mom nodded, holding my arm tight. "Okay, well, do you want to lead the way, or?" She left the question dangling, waiting for Jeanine to fill in the blank.

I hated when she did that to me. Like I should know the answer and I better say the right thing.

Jeanine avoided our eyes. She flicked her gaze around our heads and off into the trees somewhere behind us. A slight shrug and she swallowed. "I'm going to stay in case any more show up. I would hate for anyone to miss out on being in camp because I wasn't here, you know?" She cleared her throat and shifted her feet, the rustle distinct in the shadows.

Glancing around the small clearing, Mom stepped backwards, dragging me with her. I would've protested verbally, but she glared my way.

Eyes piercing, Jeanine watched every move we made. She shuffled our way, pursing her lips. "I could walk back with you and return right after." She didn't back down, like a Kirby salesman in our neighborhood a few weeks ago. What did she have to sell though? What did she care if we went with her?

We held our ground, a small standoff and I wasn't quite sure what the reward was. Mom acquiesced with a nod. "Sure, why don't you lead? I've never been to Larry's. Isn't it close by?"

"Yeah, not far actually." Offering a too-bright smile, Jeanine turned, tugging at the hem of her shirt. She moved ahead by almost twenty feet, leading the way as we slowly fell in behind her.

I leaned close to Mom and whispered. "Who's Charlie?" The name stood out to me from a memory of Mom coming home from a co-op meeting and her ranting about a man named Charlie. But that's all I remembered.

She held her whisper under the crackle of our footsteps. "He's a cruel man who fought for control of the group so much, they almost kicked him out." Mom watched Jeanine and our surroundings, her face tight.

"Why didn't they?" I stepped over a moss-laden log, rich in greens and browns. Not a trace of the smoke had reached that far north. A sweet earthy scent filled the air.

"Because Charlie had the most money invested and they couldn't kick him out without him taking every cent back or even demanding a percentage of the properties purchased. He tied himself so tightly into the financial holdings…" She shrugged, careful to hold me back from walking ahead of her. "The arguments weren't pretty when Larry joined the group. With the most land and money, he'd guaranteed himself a spot when he volunteered his place for the final camp."

How and when and where, not to mention what, Mom spent her money on after Dad and Braden died altered completely from before. She stockpiled a food storage as well as money in weapons and first aid supplies. One wouldn't think so, but each of our packs was designed to keep us alive for over three months with carefully assigned supplies.

The trail Jeanine led us down hadn't been traveled much in the past. Long grasses, shiny green on one side and silver on the other, rubbed at our pant legs. I stumbled on a protruding root, the gnarled wood bent and curved hooked my boot and grabbed me under. Mom grasped my arm again, steadying me.

I shrugged her off. "I'm okay, thanks." She patted my shoulder, checking behind us. "Who do you know that will be there?"

"I'm not sure. Jeanine didn't tell me who else." She glanced at our leader, wrinkling her brow. "Weird. Jeanine never struck me as someone to do anything others told her to do. She always seemed like the type to do her own thing." She waved her hand, as if brushing off her comment.

Whether Jeanine opposed Mom's opinion of her or not, we continued following. I'm not sure if that was a good thing or not.

CHAPTER 8

We didn't travel far before Jeanine stopped where the trail widened and curved.

She watched behind us as we closed the distance. Our breathing patterns matched, mine and Mom's, I'm not sure why but this irritated me more.

I wiped my brow. I didn't like being mad at her. Since Dad died, I wanted to be closer to Mom but she clung harder to her God, pushing me out.

Except not.

She always wanted me to pray with her, go to church with her, read scriptures with her. She wanted to pull me in, drink the Kool-Aid.

But I didn't want to do any of the stuff she based her happiness on. I had the hardest time believing anything so simple would solve all my problems.

Jeanine smiled tightly. "You don't have much further to go. I need to get back to the clearing. We're hoping more of us are just late getting in." She crossed her arms, dropping one hand from the tight self-embrace. She fiddled with a string from her jacket edge.

Mom didn't reply, stepping around Jeanine. She continued walking. Behind her, I walked further onto the flattened grass blades and didn't look at the woman.

A whiff of cheap drug store perfume slapped me across the face like she arched her arm through the air, accosting the freshness of the outdoors. The scent's presence couldn't be more out of place.

We walked on.

I'd never been up so far north. Usually Mom went to the meetings by herself. At least, I never attended one. She could have taken someone else with her. The more time I spent with Mom, the more I realized I didn't know her quite the way I thought I did.

Murmurs carried on the breeze, rustling through leaves and branches. I quickened my pace to push myself closer to my mom. I didn't need to get too far behind. Plus, I was scared out of my flipping blistering boots. Staying near Mom dulled the edge of my fear, diminishing the fright enough my pride didn't hurt so badly.

She ducked under a spindly low-hanging branch. "Sounds like the camp's right up this way. Stay close, okay? Remember, we don't trust anyone."

At least she hadn't said pray. Her usual go-to, the answer for everything. I once asked her a question about what classes to take, her answer? Pray. What should I do over the weekend? Pray. Should I get a job? Pray.

Pray. Pray. Pray.

Always. I'm supposed to pray like asking her isn't enough. What does praying do? Not bring my dad back. Praying didn't keep my brother from dying. I'm sure the world had plenty of people praying for safety and wow, the entire earth still went to hell via priority mail.

At least she went with *don't trust anyone*.

Anyone.

These people she chose to shack up with could be classified as *anyone*. Confusion set in.

We probably shouldn't be going in. If she didn't trust them, why stay? Certainly we could do better than having to watch our backs all the time. But I trusted *her* – even as I wanted to yell at her. Telling her my fears wouldn't hurt anyone.

Reaching for her shoulder, I ducked under the same branch but my jaw dropped. Entering the tightly maintained property boundaries, I swallowed. Large wall tents lined the further edge of the fenced off yard. Six foot cedar planks fenced about two football fields worth of acreage.

Jeanine had led us to the front entry path which brought us through the gate left open. Planted directly in front of the opening, we didn't have to be all the way inside to view the camp.

My fingers clenched around Mom's upper arm, digging in for stability. I couldn't drag my eyes from the compound. I held my lips still while whispering as softly as possible. "I think we should go, Mom. You don't even trust these guys. Please, let's go."

A soft shake of her head stomped my fear into a tight cement rock in my gut. "I invested too much to give up on this now. We'll be able to survive here. They have all the resources. I don't need to trust anyone to use them."

What did I say? I prayed about leaving? She'd know I was lying. Fatigue pulled at me, aching in my muscles.

A man approached from around the edge of the white gate. Dressed in a brown-and-white flannel shirt over dirty blue jeans, he offered a cautious friendly smile, eyes shifting along

Mom's frame. Taking in every detail, he held out a hand to her. "Megan, it's been a while."

Mom's shoulders stiffened. She returned the handshake but pushed back with her other hand on my waist. "Charlie. I didn't expect to see you."

His smile widened enough to reveal large canine teeth my brother used to call vampire biters. Charlie's had a peculiar dominance while the front four of his top teeth seemed smaller than most men's. "Jeanine didn't tell you I was here? Yeah, Larry didn't... make it. Come in. I have the perfect place for you and your family." He waved us inside the fence line, angling his head behind us and scanning the forest.

I stepped back toward the path. Something about his narrowed eyes and snakelike tongue flicking over his lips freaked me out. He eyed my mom the way Mr. Nelson, the baseball coach, had stared at the cheerleaders of the high school. Like she was on his menu and he couldn't wait to devour her.

"Is this everyone? Two girls out on their own can't be very safe. Come in where there's protection and we can talk. Some things have changed since the last meeting." His grin didn't reach his eyes and he motioned with his hand, holding his arm aloft as he waited for us to walk across the invisible property line connected on either end by four by four cedar posts. "I think you'll find them improvements."

Tension set minute hairs of my neck on end. We waited for what felt like another day when suddenly Mom jerked her head up and down and reached for my arm. "Okay, lead the way."

What the heck? *Don't trust anyone* just turned into *do whatever it takes to get into a group*. I shook my head, ignoring of course the constant glances Charlie threw over his shoulder at my mom.

As we walked over the closely trimmed grass, I studied my mom like a guy might. I had my experience with the boys at school. Most were perverts and didn't hide their sick thoughts as they murmured comments when they passed or accidentally bumped into the girls during the day.

Mom's hair had a thick darkness which cradled individual silver strands past her shoulders. She'd taken her ponytail down earlier and soft curls draped above the straps on her backpack. She didn't look like a woman who had kids and let herself go. Instead, Mom had a habit of treating everything in her life like it would help with her survival. Exercise and healthy eating were the best way to prepare for the end of the world. Mom always said losing weight wasn't the best way to approach the hunger of desperate times.

She fit her jeans well and had a curviness to her hips which marked her as a mom. I'd always been jealous of her curves. I still had boy hips and wouldn't mind if I got hers genetically at some point.

Smoke scented the breeze with a campfire flavor of cooking meat and charred wood. Off to our right, red bricks framed in a Volkswagen-sized pit where orange flames flickered but didn't roar. Two women clipped clothing to a wire stretched between two straight posts, decidedly devoid of expression.

We didn't stop in any of the hunting-style tents set up like summer camp cabins. Which begged the question, where were the camp counselors? Like some terrible twist on a horror flick.

Charlie strode forward with his arms swinging firmly at his sides, gaze straight ahead. He could've been checking out things in front of him, but his head didn't move side to side. He didn't strike me as a man who handled others being in charge.

The sick turning in my gut increased and I bit my inner cheek. Mom wouldn't let anything happen to us.

A house commandeered the north side of the property still inside the fence line. Charlie didn't hesitate at the steps up the porch. Nor did he pause to knock or ring a doorbell. He shoved the door open and stepped to the side to wave us in.

I shot one last glance behind me toward the direction of the now-closing gate before he shut the door.

"We'll be more comfortable in the sitting room." He tucked his hands in his pocket and winked at my mom. She jerked her head down and then glanced back at me.

How did I know things were about to get ugly? A hint could be in the slow saunter he adopted as he established the home as his. Or the continuous once-overs he stole of my mom. Something creeped me out about him and I couldn't swallow, my mouth dry from nerves.

Gripping my backpack straps, I followed Mom across the foyer and into a sitting room decorated with dead animal heads mounted above a mantle with paisley printed couches and coffee tables spotted with water rings. I chewed on the inner skin of my cheek with more ferocity. Why were we here? Why hadn't we left yet?

Inside, I was screaming. But outside? I was going along with Mom. Stuck.

Charlie motioned toward the couches. I didn't want to sit. They looked like the type of furniture stereotypical pedophiles would have. Lifetime shows on Saturday afternoons had taught me to be weary of anyone with overly patterned sofas and unfeminine accents.

We sat, but gingerly like the couches hid hunting traps beneath their cushions, ready to spring at our butt cheeks. I hadn't walked as far as I had for my butt to get eaten off by a dang couch – in paisley for crying out loud. I didn't bother hiding my glare as Charlie claimed his own seat beside the river rock fireplace.

He steepled his hands and pressed his fingers to his mouth, drawing out the moment like a poorly written suspense novel. Speak already. He lowered his hands to rest on his lap and inclined his head. "Megan, you didn't bring your husband. Is he coming later?"

I squinted at my mom, anxious for her to lie. Say anything to keep Dad's invisible protection wrapped around us.

"My husband and my son are dead." Her short answer surprised me. I'd never heard her speak so clipped. She smiled while speaking – maybe to take the edge off her tone?

Charlie crossed his arms, his smile broadening. "I'm sorry to hear that."

"Thank you." Skimming the room with her eyes, she reached down and scratched at her ankle beneath the top of her boot. "So can we go to our tent? I believe I'm supposed to have the one on the far end."

Shrugging, Charlie leaned back, piercing her with his stare. "Well, rules have changed, Megan. You don't have a man to protect you. Those are needed here. Without a protector, you can't have a tent to yourself." He spread his hands, palms out with fingers fanned. "The rule was not created for fun, but more for safety. I'm sure you understand."

"Protection? I don't need a man to protect me, Charlie. You know this. We took the same classes. I have a carry concealed license. You've seen me shoot." She clenched her jaw. Mom held herself together, but barely.

Charlie stilled, like he sensed a blow up might be inevitable, if he didn't take care with his next word selections. "I'm not questioning your skills. What the protection rule prevents is the men taking what they want, because someone is responsible for that woman or…" He pointed my way. "family."

"I think my gun will be able to protect us from any of the men. Why are those kind of men allowed in this camp, if they can't be trusted to act civilized?" Mom's eyebrow arched and I lifted mine. She only asked questions when she knew the answer.

"Oh, about that. I'm going to need you to turn your weapons in. People can't run around with guns in the camp. That can't be safe for anyone, especially if an unfortunate accident occurs." He offered a condescending smile – a match to my gym teacher's grin when she told us we weren't required to run but we had to make a time limit on the mile – exactly low enough to require us to run.

Mom stared at Charlie. She didn't waver.

He met her gaze, unflinching. "Listen, I don't have anyone claimed myself. You and your daughter can stay in the house with me. You just be… available… and you'll have protection in the camp." He pointed at me. "Her too. It's really that easy."

"And if I want to leave?" Mom lifted her chin, squaring her jaw. Finally, her logical side kicked in. *Let's go!*

"You should've gone before coming inside. Now that you've entered our walls, you're community responsibility. We can't afford for you to leave. So you can either stay with me, protected, or you can take your chances in a community tent." Charlie's smile didn't change, but the skin around his eyes hardened. He pointed toward Mom's bruised and scraped face. "Looks like you already experienced a taste of what's out there as it is. Congratulations escaping, but do you think you'll do so well next time?"

I clenched my knees together, curling my toes. He wasn't a man I wanted to be caught alone with. He took a positive and slanted it into doubt.

Mom's lips parted. Pure shock slackened her features. She didn't speak. I'm sure she couldn't. His proposition reeked and I'm not surprised she couldn't figure out what to say.

He continued. "I'll need to know what other skills you have to benefit the group. Your value will adjust what your standing is with us, when you eat, when your lookout times are, and so on." He thrummed his fingers on his upper thigh, glancing from me to Mom.

"But... But everything was already decided. Our positions were established and now you're changing them? I don't understand." Mom dug her fingers into the material above her knee.

Charlie didn't drop his grin. "I know it's confusing, but when management changes other things do, too."

"I can still protect myself and my daughter." Mom stiffened her lip. I had no doubt her stubbornness alone would keep us safe and fed and even thriving – with or without a group to support us.

Fingers shaped into a gun, index pointed at me, Charlie cocked his jaw to the side. "What about her? Think you can protect her, twenty-four hours? When you're sleeping? When she needs to use the restroom? Choose me and I'll keep you on the same rotations, same shifts. Don't... and, well." He shrugged, picking at the cuticle on his thumb. His sudden disinterest alarmed me more than his threats.

So what if he couldn't promise Mom anything. She could. She brought us to the group. She had to be able to trust some of those people, right? If not, what were we doing there?

Mom didn't speak. I watched them and looked around wildly, his words, their meaning terrifying, but I couldn't grasp why. Yes, his threat was clear. But would that horror be allowed in a community designed for safety? I was too tired, too confused. Too out of my element to understand exactly what was being thrown down and how it had happened to us.

Charlie's voice lowered. He leaned forward conspiratorially. "Look, think of it this way. You control if it's voluntary or not, if it's more than just me. More importantly, your daughter will be protected by more than you alone. It's like we'll be working together to keep her safe."

Mom waited another drawn out thirty seconds before nodding her head.

She ignored the caveat to the promise in his tone.

The promise which said we'd be protected.

For now.

CHAPTER 9

Charlie's control slipped around Mom and I like an old-fashioned corset. Tightening slowly but firmly with inexorable pressure.

He placed us in a bedroom along the back of the house. Claiming none of the others had bathrooms, he proceeded to tell us to use the outhouse along the southern fence line.

Mom avoided my questioning glare.

Standing beside the door, Mom fiddled with the zipper on her sweatshirt. Charlie stopped in front of her, their height difference extremely apparent as he bent his head to look down at her.

Mom squared her jaw, lifting her chin with stubbornness I recognized all too well.

He brushed a strand of hair from her face. Her cheek twitched. He murmured. "My room's right next door. I'll see you tonight." Charlie glanced my way and dropped his hand. "Dinner is in shifts. I'll talk to Murray about adding you to the second shift with me." And then he was gone, leaving an oily residue in the air behind him.

Silent as a breeze pushing through the woods, Mom closed the door. She swung her bag onto the bed and sighed.

Knock. Knock.

The sound echoed with the wooden floor acoustics.

We froze. Now what?

Mom crossed to the door and opened the panel partway.

Charlie's profile bobbed in and out of my field of view in the line of the slim opening. His low murmur burned my ears. "Megan, you need to give me your gun." He cleared his throat. "I'll keep it in my room. No one else will have access to it, okay?"

Mom's hand flew to the holster at the small of her back. Reflexively, she wrapped her fingers around the handle. "This is my only one. I can't just give it to you."

But it wasn't the only gun. Mom had a smaller weighted one sewn into the bottom of my pack. Not only was she lying, she was convincing. Since when did my mom lie?

Charlie paused, the one eye I could see narrowed. "If you don't give it to me, I'll be forced to take it. That's no way to start off together, is it?"

Together? Who did he think he was? Mom's husband? Creep.

She shook her head, the movement small and graceful. With extreme care, she unsnapped the strap securing her gun and withdrew the piece at a finite pace. Slipping the butt of her gun into his hand, Mom stared at her offering as if her last tank of oxygen slipped away.

With his empty hand, Charlie patted my mom's head. Like a stupid dog! I ground my teeth. Mom closed the door as he turned and walked away.

A sick twist of her lips could've passed as a frown or a self-defeating smile. She didn't hesitate as she grabbed my pack and turned it over. A red tab sewn into the lining poked from the seam. Tearing the tab back, Mom pulled the entire panel open and thrust her hand inside the pocket. While she retrieved the smaller gun, she studied the room and what was available.

Inspecting it myself, I couldn't help lifting my shoulders in defeat. The sparse contents offered little in the way of comfort or style. A double bed pushed against the plain white wall had a fitted sheet and a raggedy red and blue quilt. No pillows to rest heads on. The window didn't have any fittings and the hardwood flooring lacked rugs or anything to even remotely add some character.

After reclosing the panel with the pre-installed Velcro strips, Mom palmed the gun and turned toward the closet, if that's what a medicine cabinet sized cupboard could be called. Pulling open the door, she angled herself around and walked backwards into the space.

"You're not going to fit in there." I pulled my eyebrows together. What was she doing? Sometimes Mom had a mind of her own and I couldn't follow her best-laid plans for anything. Dad used to say she had the mind of an engineer.

Raising her arms, she stretched and then carefully lowered her hands, keeping her eyes on the corner above the closet door. She wiggled out of the tight space.

With empty hands.

"Wha—" My question was interrupted by another knock at the door.

Charlie didn't wait for an invite or an answer. He pushed right in with his too-toothy grin. Another man with reddish-brown hair and a gray speckled beard followed him. The new man didn't smile, his mouth was completely covered by beard. I guess I could've missed the friendly gesture under all his facial hair, but his eyes had a hard tilt to them, suggesting he hadn't smiled in a long time.

"We need to do a search of your items for any other weapons. I'm sure you understand." Charlie folded his arms and leaned against the wall separating his room from ours. "This is Sarge. He usually graces the west wall. But he didn't have anything else going on. He'll be checking your things. If you'll come over here." He spoke pleasantly enough, but the clip to each word confirmed he wouldn't take anything less than complete cooperation.

The room wasn't large enough for us to move far, so the shuffling to adjust ourselves closer to him only increased the awkwardness of the moment. Mom positioned herself between Charlie and myself. She folded her hands and held them discreetly at her waist.

I copied her. Mom had a calm assuredness about her I found more comforting than any amount of words would be.

Charlie turned and faced us, ignoring his man's rough handling of our things. "I didn't get a chance to formally meet your daughter, Megan." He left his comment hanging with a loud unspoken 'introduce us, now' in the air.

Pasting on her fake-I'm-going-to-puke-on-you-when-I-get-the-chance smile, Mom nodded my direction. "This is Kelly. Kelly, this is Charlie Penderson."

He smiled at me, extending his hand. "Nice to officially meet you." He waited for me to return the shake which I did with firmness. My dad hadn't shirked on raising me. Charlie nodded. "Good grip. How old are you, Kelly?" His voice and the sincerity of his eyes betrayed his words – or maybe it was the other way around. I could see how he was so easy to trust, to follow.

Mom put her arm around me and squeezed, breaking the connection Charlie had allowed to continue past the societal norm. "Kelly just turned twelve. Isn't she tall?" She kissed my forehead and something in her eyes told me to keep my mouth shut and go along.

I grinned like an idiot and blushed. "Mo-om. I'm not that tall."

Glancing between Mom and me, Charlie's over-exuberance toward me faded. "Yes, you are tall, but you look like your mom. I never would've guessed twelve. Maybe fifteen?" He winked, turning toward Sarge who had flipped my backpack upside down and fingered the panel on the bottom.

Charlie moved forward. "What's this for, Megan?" He took the bag from Sarge's fingers and turned to Mom. "Looks like you're trying to hide something." He studied her face and her movements, like she was going to tell him everything or he was going to make her.

Mom crossed her arms over her stomach and shook her head. "Was there anything inside? I created the panel for Kelly to put any pictures or special items. We had to leave before we grabbed anything of meaning, you know? In mine there's a Bible." She pointed indifferently toward her as-yet-untouched pack.

Turning toward hers, Charlie stared for a long while at the bag, while he groped mine. A pensive twist to his head didn't reassure me about the encounter. He was too oily, too good at running people. I hadn't even known him for an hour and I could already tell he took himself more seriously than other people did.

This scared me.

I reached for my mom's hand. My movement caught Charlie's attention and he turned his stare on me. I didn't flinch. I hadn't done anything. I hadn't hidden anything in the pockets or in the room.

Sarge moved forward, upending Mom's bag and emptying her contents onto the bed as well. At least their inconsiderate nature hadn't extended so far they dropped stuff on the floor. He ripped open the bottom panel and Mom's

Bible thunked when hitting the hardwood flooring. Okay, never mind. I gave Sarge credit too soon.

Charlie knelt, retrieving the book and gazing at Mom while he rose. "You weren't kidding. You never spoke of your religion at the co-op."

"What I believe is nobody's business." How could Mom speak so calmly, even with a dash of attitude? The men in that room weren't our friends. They weren't there to help us. They wanted to do exactly what the government had done before my dad had left for the south. Taken a vote and created a buy-sell-trade mentality for gun owners and their neighbors.

If a person owned a gun, they were expected to buy a license, giving their weapon a documented address. Refusal to do so would require them to sell their weapons. If neither of those steps were done, neighbors or anyone who knew about people with guns – licensed or not – could trade information for commodities. With gas and other resources so high, need was a powerful motivator.

"Well, I disagree. We don't allow organized religion here. So don't start preaching or anything. I'll hold onto your Bible in my room, so you don't get any ideas." He dropped my bag and reached forward to pat Mom's stiff shoulder.

"You don't need it anyway. Can't you see? God's already forgotten you." He jerked his fingers at Sarge and they tromped toward the door and disappeared without looking back.

I turned back to Mom, angry they took her Bible but also slightly vindicated someone else agreed with me on the whole religion thing. There was nothing comforting about *who* agreed with me.

She slumped onto the bed, her hands shaking as she reached for our things. Shirts and pants sifted through her fingers and she didn't even grasp for them.

"Mom, are you okay?" The guys hadn't been overly threatening, more irritating and oily, but not scary. Tears in her eyes when she lifted her gaze to mine made my stomach wring in worry. What had I missed? Why wasn't I crying? If Mom was worried or upset, something was bad enough to be concerned about.

"You did a great job hiding the gun. I'm sure you can get your other one back." I lamely lifted my hand, letting fall back to my side when my words failed.

She barely shook her head and looked down into her lap. Her lips moved, but I couldn't hear her. A large tear dripped onto her pants.

I moved to sit beside her, pushing a pile of things across the mattress. "I didn't hear you." My fingers fiddled with the lower zipper on my outer jacket. My family wasn't big on hugging and for the first time in my life, I wondered why.

She sniffed, wiping at her cheeks. "He took my Bible. That was… cruel."

"Mom, I'm sorry. I know. Try to think of it as just a book. He didn't take anything else." I tried not to sigh. She was upset over the book. He didn't take our last gun, which I thought was a small victory. I nudged her shoulder. "We didn't know he would take that or we could've hidden the Bible too. He didn't even think to check the rest of the room."

She stared at me, disappointment shiny in another tear slipping through her defenses. The skin around her swollen and bruised eye tightened and flushed under her tears. "Kelly, you're going to fit in here too fast, if you can believe all he took was a book."

Her comment stung. I recoiled, blinking rapidly at the sudden verbal attack. "Mom, I didn't deserve that. In the whole scheme of things, it *was* just a book. What do you want me to say?" But it wasn't. I knew it wasn't. But if I could downplay the book's relevance, than maybe it wouldn't be so obvious that I was glad that her *book* was all he'd taken. I could hide my fear a little longer.

"I want you to keep your childish opinions to yourself. That *book* is a foundation of beliefs. Whether you have a religious attachment to it or not the connotation in that *book* is understood by everyone. He took my Bible as a power play. Charlie wants to control us – me. He proved he can *take* anything he wants. *Do* anything he wants." She pushed off the mattress and stood, spinning to thrust loose items into her pack.

"Childish? You might still see me as twelve, but I'm seventeen. I have a more developed idea of what's going on than you might think." I copied her actions. She wasn't the only one in a difficult situation. I thrust random shirts and socks into the depths of my pack. "Why'd you say I'm twelve anyway?" Was I so innocent acting? So naïve?

She threw the last of her things inside her bag and turned to me, her jaw tight. "Don't you understand what's going on here? He just claimed me as his own. If I didn't go along with his stupid rule, he all but promised me we would both be raped. As long as you act like you're twelve, we might be able to save you from being claimed by anyone else. Do you understand, now?"

She looked me over, anger heating her normal professional cool. "You keep your chest wrapped and don't tell anyone. This isn't some game or a practice drill. This is reality now, Kelly.

You don't have the luxury of hiding behind me anymore in your disbelief." She poked her finger into the air inches from my face. "You need to start paying attention."

I didn't flinch as her words hailed around me. Twelve? Binding my breasts would keep them hidden but was I really so immature looking I would pass for five years younger? Holding my face blank wouldn't have been possible, if I were twelve. The snarky comments didn't pass my lips. Confrontation with my mother never went well. She had an ability to not get as worked up as I did and usually watched as I went from this-is-what's-making-me-mad to complete and uncontrollable meltdown because of her serenity.

While she packed fast, I took my time. The longer I worked on picking up, the less I would have to deal with her. I wonder if I could pack for a year.

CHAPTER 10

Apparently the camp announced dinner shift with a bell, the first round of diners called with one ding.

When the bell sounded, I grabbed my full pack and flung it to the floor, kicking the bag into the corner. As much as the sandwiches we hadn't eaten looked appealing, I needed something more filling.

Mom knelt in prayer almost twenty minutes ago. No talking or other sound between us but the huffing of our breath, until she stood when I turned the door handle.

"You can't leave, Kelly. You don't know anyone here. I'm not sure if we can even count on the ones I thought I knew. I have no idea how these people are going to act." She didn't move other than to point toward the rest of the house and compound.

I leaned my forehead against the door. "Are you kidding me?" Pausing for a moment, I stared at the simple white lines of the grain of the wood. Finally, I gave in to the rush of anger and disbelief swelling over me. I spun, hurt beyond measure. "Then why are we here? What are we doing? We can do this on our own. I know we can. Let's go. If you don't trust them, then why?"

She rushed to me, pushing the air at waist height with her flat, opened hand. "Shh. Shh. Shh. You have to keep your voice down. They need to think we trust them." She didn't speak in a whisper, but more of a hushed, library tone. "You were at the same meeting I was. Didn't you hear what he said? Come on, Kelly."

We stared at each other. So many things unsaid. Too many to get over with a simple conversation. I wanted to cry out, loud as I could, and beg her to leave.

"You're going to sleep with Charlie so I'm safe? We're staying here because he *said* we can't leave. How do we know if we haven't even tried?" How could she not understand what was wrong with that? "We don't need them." If I gave her the benefit of the doubt, I could imagine she didn't understand the bully mentality. But that wasn't going to work when she was getting raped that evening. "No matter how voluntary you go with him tonight, it's still rape, Mom."

"I know that, Kelly. But can't you see that at least it's just me, and not you too?" She pressed her heated face close to mine, eyes searching, pleading with me to understand.

"We need to leave. Leave now. Please, Mom." I couldn't offer her understanding. How was I supposed to go along with her sacrifice when it only protected something as simple as my virginity?

"Where would we go? This place is everything I've been preparing for. Trust me, no one will survive out *there* by themselves. I've done the research and people don't survive outside of a group." Adamantly shaking her head, she turned to the window and the paper-thin curtains.

I folded my arms. Could that be true? I tried to recall any American history from school or anything I might have read to refute her claim, but any historical classes had culled out anything earlier than the 1980s and pop culture. Except for the last few years when the wars had started.

No, the teachers and administrators loved to replay the media blitzes of most of the Middle East disappearing under nukes while Asia, northern Europe, and the southern countries turned on each other.

The most famous of memes had been one where the American flag had been depicted sitting in a throne while all the other flags had fought below it, tearing each other apart. The caption had said, "Why fight, when they'll do it for you?"

After surviving their own skirmishes, the leaders of the remaining countries had turned on the USA. Good ole US. I couldn't remember any lesson mentioning the first two World Wars, and there had to be a One and a Two because they referred to this one as Three. To have a third there had to have been a previous two, right? Humanity survived those, we had a chance with this one, too. Right?

All information about anything other than approved "facts" was destroyed. Even on the internet access to anything pre-1980s required mad skills in the hacking department because most of the time the information was a ghost of what it used to be. I had only been ten when the internet had become "controllable."

So Mom could spout off her facts and I would never know. I would never be the wiser, because my education didn't encompass everything hers did. Hers was the lucky generation.

"I can volunteer then. You don't need to do it. Everything about tonight will go against your beliefs and I don't have any preconceived notions on any of it." I laughed at myself. "I'm even a virgin still, for crying out loud. Why should you get to have all the fun before we die?" My lips tight, I refused to cry. What the heck were we doing? Talking about which of us would get raped that night to stay in a camp we didn't feel safe in.

Mom whirled to me, arms outstretched as she pulled me to her chest. "No. I don't care how mad at me you are. What happens tonight isn't how anyone should be treated. We can't leave. He all but promised me they wouldn't let us go."

Wouldn't let us go? Great. That made me feel so much better about staying. I hung my head, reaching up to rub my forehead. "Fine. Can we go eat, now?" Starved, I wasn't only hungry for food, but for conversation with people outside of my reality. Talking with someone who had different information or even a different perception, I might be able to feel a modicum of normalcy. Because I couldn't help feeling like I had been slammed into a horrible role-playing bit and no one had given me a script.

"Charlie said we'll be eating with the second shift. If they at least left the dining rules alone, the first bell is for the first diners. We'll wait here for the second." She sank to the mattress, folding her hands in her lap. Demure, her countenance seemed fake after such a fired up encounter. "We could pray for comfort?" She made the suggestion like a question, like I would want to pray for anything.

Ignoring her, I jerked my thumb toward the door. "I need to use the bathroom. Can I do that?"

She reclaimed her feet, moving to stand beside me. "I'll go with you. I don't know how this works, this claiming or protection thing. They've changed so much. Barbarianism never made sense." Mom touched my arm, forcing me to meet her gaze. "I'm serious, Kelly. Don't tell anyone your age. If you can't act twelve, keep quiet, okay?"

Nodding, if not to agree, then certainly to get us going out the door, I needed to get a lay of the area. If I couldn't count on Mom to get us out, I had to try myself.

~~~

Dinner turned out to be warmed refried beans and a poor attempt at homemade tortillas.

The second shift consisted of Charlie, Mom, me, and three other men who spoke like they suspected "Big Brother" still monitored everyday things. The government could have taken things back and control reigned everywhere but in the crap camp.

We sat at a long, rough wood picnic table with attached benches like those at a public park. I sat across from Mom and picked up the simple salt shaker. Beneath the cardboard cylinder, a black brand claimed the table as Farragut State Park Property. Which guy or guys had stolen the table? How many other things had been taken before the fallout?

Someone who stole when things were safe had the potential for so much worse with danger shoved in their face.

The grass had been tamped down in the area by a lot of feet. Camp population hadn't been very evident when we arrived. Two women and a couple men was all, if I remembered correctly.

A man to our left grunted to the guy across from him. "This isn't something that could've been prevented."

My ears perked up. I rolled the tortilla slowly, careful to take a bite and chew soft enough I could hear but not so slow I looked stupid.

"You don't think with a little less arrogance and a lot more service, we could have avoided being bombed?" The second man put his burrito down and stared at the man across from him.

The other guy shrugged, avoiding eye contact in a more pacifist stand. "I think we could've protected ourselves better, if the president didn't position all our troops in other countries and the National Guard on the borders. Fat lot of good the soldiers did anyone when illegals attacked from both sides. You can't fight a dual-sided ambush." He bit into his tortilla wrap, careful to keep eyes focused on his dinner.

Thumping the table, Man Number Two spluttered. "We should be helping others. Everyone was destroying each other. We had to help those lower countries."

Slowly, the first man stopped chewing and swallowed. He met the other man's stare. His face flushed while his eyes moistened. "They weren't destroyed and now we are." He shoved the rest of his burrito in his mouth and left the table.

The second man's shoulders slumped, but he resumed eating.

Mom leaned over, reaching for the ketchup bottle. "You okay, Tom?"

Heaving a sigh, Tom stole a peek at Mom. "Thanks, Megan. He's new, but his ideas are strong and he's a good worker." Tom flitted his gaze around the immediate encampment.

Charlie and the other men stood at the drink station and didn't spare us a second's worth of attention. He lowered his voice to a whisper. "Watch your back. Things aren't like we planned, in case you haven't noticed yet." He held his gaze trained on the men. "They say one thing but have two more planned behind the door. These guys are evil."

I bit into my burrito again, absorbing the tension crackling on the air around me.

Mom sipped her water and muttered under the cup brim. "What else is going on? Have you heard anything?"

Tom shook his head, but watched his plate. "Mostly what we expected, except Russia didn't bomb us. They're out. Apparently, England took them. China and most of Asia is gone. Australia's out. The only three countries besides the US left – if the US is left – are rumored to be UK, Poland, and Germany, if you can believe that."

Three. Such a small number considering a week ago the whole first world had been intact. Third-world countries had disappeared under the Protective Wars last summer.

Rolling a second burrito, Tom leaned in for a bite. His lips moved the edge of the flour wrap with his words. "I'm not sure what's going on here. Between us, you might be smart to find a way to move on."

I couldn't keep the small smile from my lips as I bit into the soft dinner. At least someone else – no, at least an adult had the same thoughts as me. Now Mom would have to see me as someone to take seriously. No matter what she wanted others to believe.

Mom opened her mouth to counter but Tom cleared his throat and took another bite, looking down.

My gaze hadn't risen above the end of my burrito, but I jumped anyway when Charlie took the seat beside Mom and draped his arm across her shoulders. "How're you girls settling in? Everything going okay?" He smirked at the other men moving in around us. "Told you guys. She's not much to look at, but she's motivated."

Wincing, I smiled and raised my plastic cup. "Are other kids here?" Internally I cringed at the sickly sweet voice I used, the tone bouncing back at me from the bottom of my cup. My mom was gorgeous. The fact that her looks had been brutalized didn't take away from her beauty.

Suddenly somber, Charlie shook his head. "No, sweetheart. The two families with children didn't reach camp in time."

Mom glanced sharply at Charlie's face. "I thought the deadline was tomorrow."

He shrugged, leaning back to stretch his legs. "No. Jeanine went back to get the last of our intel from the meetup place when you guys arrived. We're not letting anyone else in. We need our rations." He brazenly winked at me with my mom's face focused downward. "Plus, there are marauders looting and killing already as far north as Rathdrum. We can't take the chance of letting them slip through our defenses. We're taking today and tomorrow to seal up any possible weak spots in the perimeter."

She finished her burrito, her eyes tight.

The creepy sensation around him intensified. How could she handle his arm around her? No other kids in camp? Who was I supposed to talk to?

~~~

I don't know what I expected for our first night in camp – campfire burning surrounded by a circle of people talking and roasting marshmallows or something. Certainly not Sarge claiming the men from dinner for a perimeter check, while Mom and I returned to our room to wait for Charlie.

Sitting Indian-style on the hard floor across from the bed, I leaned against the wall. Mom knelt by the bed, but she didn't bow her head. Instead she lifted her face, as if beseeching the heavens – or the ceiling. I'm not sure.

Knock, knock.

Our heads whipped toward the door. Mom's shoulders hunched when she stood. She straightened them as if making a decision. She didn't look at me.

The knock had come from the adjoining door.

Suddenly, harshness of the reality hit me in the face. I looked at the ground.

Mom had never loved another man besides my father. She'd never been touched by anyone else. With her faith, she believed in chastity and marriage. Devout loyalty.

I didn't want a martyr for a mother, yet she padded past me, her steps short and sure.

She faltered at the door. We didn't look at each other, but I sat inches from the frame. I reached out and squeezed her foot. Whispering, I stared at the grains in the flooring. "Mom, we can leave. Let's go. Don't do this."

"You won't be safe anywhere, Kel. You heard him talk about the marauders. That's gangs, Kelley. I can at least do my best here. Don't let anyone through the other door." Her whisper barely reached me and she turned the handle, slipping through the doorway like a portal.

A portal which didn't block out sound.

The low murmur of Charlie's voice and a discordant rising and falling of his tone frightened me. I scooted toward the foot of the bed, staring at the gap under the door. The increasing darkness hadn't bothered me until that exact moment.

What if someone did try to come through the hallway door while she was gone? Tom had warned us about the men there. I couldn't stand fast enough. Trying to push out the thoughts of what Mom had to do in Charlie's bedroom so that we – no, I – could stay safe, I turned the lock on the door and rushed back to the bed.

Nothing would get me out of my clothes. I crawled across the comforter and lay down, pressing myself against the cool paint of the wall.

His voice only sounded distant, not more muffled or even – what I really wanted – gone.

And like that twelve-year-old I was supposed to be, I plugged my ears with a finger in each and hummed softly to myself.

I eventually fell asleep like a child hiding from a thunderstorm.

~~~

When I woke I wasn't in my bed at home with the realization everything had been a dream.

No, I woke when the door between the rooms creaked open then clicked shut. I stared at the wall in the gray of the night while my mom crossed the floor. I waited for the bed to dip with her weight, but it never did.

Her restrained sobs rocked the bed softly. A slight shaking from the end of the mattress suggested she leaned on the foot.

I lifted my head carefully to check on her.

Simple moonlight spilled through the window revealing my mother's kneeling form at the foot of the bed. Her folded hands steepled above her head. She hid her face as she cried into the blanket.

While I had been angry at Mom, sad about Dad and Braden, and confused about the whole war and escape thing – even as prepared as we were – an emotion I hadn't had to deal with consumed me.

Hate.

I have never hated anyone. Or anything.

Right there, as I lay in that bed, my hatred encompassed Charlie.

And God.

CHAPTER 11

The next morning I couldn't look Mom in the eye. So much had been torn from her – her Bible, her security in the group, and her belief in the people she'd worked with, all because of me.

We plaited our hair into braids, Mom's a single French down the back and mine in two different trails down the sides inches above my ears. The chill had reached our room and the cool tips of my fingers brushed my neck as I worked.

I had slept with the bindings on my chest. What if they compressed my breasts so much, I never saw them again? We were taking the whole twelve-year-old thing too far.

She didn't speak as we grabbed our toothbrushes and pulled on our sweatshirts. The sun hadn't been up long and a walk around the grounds as well as a visit to the outhouse before breakfast moved us out of bed earlier than we probably wanted. I would die before begging her to hurry. I had to use the toilet so bad I wanted to cry.

Opening the door quietly, Mom stuck her head out into the hall and waited. After less than a minute but what could have passed as eternity, she motioned me forward. I followed her, glancing back into our for-now-home before softly closing the door. I wasn't completely comfortable leaving our stuff unattended, but Mom didn't have any problems.

Windowless, the hallway's dim interior didn't register the rising sun. On the opposite end from us light illuminated the living quarters and the front door beyond. The house wasn't huge but more than comfortable for a larger family.

We tread carefully over the hardwood floor which extended throughout the remainder of the home. Passing a door, I glanced through the small opening of the ajar panel.

A man's body lay slumped over a desk. Black flies buzzed over a bloody hole in the back of his head.

I covered my mouth, smothering my gasp. Mom glanced sharply at me.

Swallowing, I shook my head and mouthed sorry. She hadn't seen. I probably wasn't meant to witness that. Who knows how long he'd been there. Since the uprising Jeanine had mentioned? Obviously there had been more violence than she'd let on. We moved past the door just as the fingers of a horrific odor stretched for us.

When would the fear stop raging through me? A normal emotion would be so nice right about then. Fear and anger had ruled me since – only a day or two ago.

Amazingly, the world had slipped into uncontrolled chaos only two days before. Two days. My life would never be normal again.

At the front door, Mom ushered me through, like she didn't want me to be the last one in the building. After the man in the office, I didn't argue or try to sidestep her maneuverings.

In the fresh early morning light, Mom and I lifted our shoulders as we breathed in. Dad had always called the move our shoulder breaths. I glanced at Mom. Did she remember that? It'd been so long ago.

She met my gaze, lifting her lip on one side. But her eyes had faded. Overnight my mom had changed. Facing the alterations in the brutally honest lighting hurt worse than if I'd taken her place last night. I reached for her hand, finding hers as she reached for mine. Our fingers clung to each other.

The outhouse had been constructed on a pier foundation and enclosed with brown painted paneling.

Groaning and creaking, the steps didn't like us as we climbed the few stairs to get to the double doors. In a ten-by-ten square, four seats had been built for people to use at once. But they weren't separated by partitions and they all accessed the same toilet paper which hung from the ceiling on a thick wire.

Over holes, plastic toilet seats screwed into place on crudely painted plywood. I pushed my lower jaw to the side and bit my lip. Tears threatened and I dashed them away as they overfilled and flowed from my eyelids. Porta-potties had always been the bane of my existence and there they were – something I'd have to live with the rest of... whatever this was.

"Let's get this over with." Mom sighed. She always hated them, too. And now we had to pee in front of each other. Oh, the stupid injustices.

The freezing cold seat, the lack of privacy, the odor of already spent waste – not one thing could be spun to a more optimistic outlook.

Except my mom and I hadn't died yet. The thought made me smile in spite of the questionable toilet paper I wrapped around my fingers.

"What's so funny?" Mom stood, pulling her pants up, but not before fresh bruises below her underwear line caught my eye.

I looked away, determined to talk to her about Charlie and our circumstances. We could still leave. Why hadn't we left?

"Trying to think of something positive and the first thought I had was we hadn't died yet." I followed her actions and stood, lowering the seat and not looking inside at other people's remains.

She paused at the door, head tilted to the side as she considered my comment. "I guess you're right."

Accepting a huffing of air from her as the closest thing to a laugh I was going to get, I stretched my arms over my head.

Outside, no one else had arisen yet. At least from where we stood. Bathrooms were usually very busy places first thing in the morning.

The meal bell tolled once, the chime melancholy. My stomach grumbled as if on cue. "What do you think we'll have for breakfast?"

"Probably oatmeal or creamed wheat. Cheapest stuff to keep on hand." She didn't lead us toward the dining area. Instead we headed to the fence-line surrounding the modest compound.

Built for permanently restricted privacy, the six-foot cedar fence surrounded the compound with determined stalwartness. Along the top of the border ran a two-foot diameter of tightly wound barbed-wire. The glaring points promised a fight and the metal cord wouldn't lose.

With my chest bound so tightly, I could run without needing to change. The idea of exercising without fleeing from something or someone sent a thrill of giddiness through me. I glanced at Mom. "Do you want to go for a run? No one is out here."

She lifted her gaze from the ground in front of us, careful to study as much of the camp as possible. After a prolonged moment where we trudged forward about twenty steps, she scrunched her nose and gave the barest head shake. "I don't think we should let them see we can run."

I grabbed her elbow, shaking her until she faced me. "Mom, why are we still here? Enough is enough. Thank you for your attempts to keep me safe. We. Don't. Need. This. Seriously. Enough." Tears pricked at my eyelids. Why was I so emotional that I couldn't even plea for freedom without losing it? "We don't trust them. They've taken our stuff. You've been... hurt... I mean come on, Mom. What are we doing?" Pausing, I allowed the silence to fill with the rustle of the tree limbs in the breeze. "My virginity isn't worth that much."

"Worth what?" She peered at me, like I knew something I wasn't saying.

"Worth the bruises. Worth what you went through last night." I lifted my jaw, challenging her to deny what I'd seen. I softened my grip. "Or the loss of your beliefs." Raising my hands like in surrender, I released her arm. "I'm not saying I share the same faith as you, I'm saying nothing is worth trading that part of you, right? If nothing else, we shouldn't give that up."

She avoided me, watching the empty grounds and forest past the fence.

I nudged her shoulder with mine. "I mean, heck, maybe you and your prayers *have* kept us alive this long." My playful laugh hid the sincerity of my words. I had no idea why we were allowed to survive. I couldn't discount the power of Mom's prayers and their potential role in keeping us alive. At some point we were destined to join Dad and Braden. Her prayers could sustain our lives there since each word was most likely built out of sheer stubbornness.

She nodded slightly and faced me. Unshed tears glistened in her eyes.

Uncomfortable with my impassioned speech to get through to her that I didn't want her getting hurt for any reason, I shifted my feet. My stomach hurt. I couldn't wait to eat – oatmeal or not.

We stamped around the fence line, careful to keep an even pace, not too fast nor too slow. I understood the concept behind keeping our strengths and weaknesses close to our chests. We didn't speak as we rounded the last hunting tent closest to the dining area.

Five women huddled in a group to the side while eight men sat and ate at the picnic tables. Dressed simply in gray cotton shirts and plain worn jeans, the women each had their arms crossed while they rubbed the tops of their arms and kind of jostled in place. The men, however, wore sweatshirts and flannels designed to ward off the chill.

At our approach, the men's conversation died off as they spotted us one by one.

A thin, reed-like man stood, his features tightly pinched together like a weasel's. "Where's your man?" He growled, his voice much lower than his body would suggest.

"My man? Are you serious, Spencer? Don't talk to me like you control me. I built this place just as much as you did – if not more. I'm here to eat with my daughter. Sit back down."

Mom's derision drenched the immediate area. Authority strengthened her tone.

Glancing at each other, the guys sitting looked more constipated than confused. Spencer worked his mouth like he'd been shot and he couldn't believe it. His face flushed and he barked at the women. "Get me more food."

One of them jumped, dropping her arms to her sides and rushing toward the portable camp stove. A huge pot cooked over a propane-fed burner, the lid at an angle while a handle protruded from the opening. The girl fumbled with the lid then replaced it. She turned and ran to Spencer to claim his bowl.

He reached down and cuffed the side of her head. "I'm waiting you stupid girl."

Mom jerked forward, then held back. She'd seen more than she wanted to. So had I.

"Well, well, you found the place." Jeanine limped gracelessly under the canopy and grinned crookedly at Mom. Her right eyebrow had been split and discolored to a gnarly purple and red mix, swelling to half-cover her eye. With her hair pulled back tightly into a ponytail which trailed down her back, Jeanine's damaged ear and bruise-covered neck were plain to see.

Mom sidled toward her, careful to keep us distanced from the men sitting at the table. Whispering, Mom leaned in to Jeanine, placing her hand on her upper biceps. "Jeanine, are you okay? What's going on? This isn't what Larry had planned. What any of us planned."

Careful to keep her expression light, Jeanine smiled brightly at Mom. She lifted her voice to encompass the group. "Let me show you where the restroom is. Sometimes, it's hard to figure things out here – since Charlie reorganized things." She smiled at the men and ignored the group of girls. "Come this way."

The last time we followed Jeanine we ended up in a camp where a control freak had taken us to stay in a small bedroom off of his with a stolen gun – who took people's things no less. Why, then, did Mom follow her so willingly? Why, too, did the men wiggle their eyebrows at Jeanine and catcall?

Over the yard, the distance to the bathroom went quickly as Jeanine picked up the pace the further from the eating area we got. She burst through the doors and slammed them shut behind us. Leaning against the panel, she slid to the floor, sobbing into her hands.

Mom flicked her gaze toward me then squatted beside the broken-down woman. "What's going on?"

Heaven help Jeanine, if she thought she wouldn't have to be straight with my mom. When

Mom used *that* tone, you answered or you got ripped a new one.

Jeanine didn't need encouragement or persuasion. Her sobs subsided enough she could lightly pant and talk. "This isn't how life after was supposed to be. Larry had everything planned perfectly. We were all friends before and then Charlie came in and shot Larry—"

"Is he the one in the office inside the house?" I grimaced at the sharp glance my mom sent me. I ducked my head. "Sorry, I didn't mean to interrupt."

Nodding, Jeanine bit her lip. "After he killed Larry, Charlie brought in new people. Spencer and Sarge totally went for it because Charlie promised them all kinds of things – like girls." She bared her teeth. "Because I can't think of any girl desperate enough to want a jerk like Spencer, and Sarge is a dumb stupid animal."

Her assessments seemed spot on. From what I'd witnessed, Jeanine had a firm grasp on the realities of the camp.

"Who did this to you?" Mom softly pushed stray strands of hair off Jeanine's face, revealing more scrapes and developing bruises along her hair line.

Jeanine raised her shaking hand to wipe at her nose, ligature marks bright red and purple on her wrists as her sleeves pulled back. "Those men and some others last night."

I gasped. What else could I do? I only ever read about the cruelty of people in banned books we'd traded behind the bleachers at school. Only a few hours into devastation and society had completely disappeared. "I thought this place was supposed to be safe, Mom. Haven't you seen enough?" People had lost all sense of decency. I grabbed her arm. "Please, we *need* to get out of here."

Clutching Mom's forearm, Jeanine pulled her close, her one eye wide and focused. "Megan, listen to your daughter. You need to get out now. In between…" She averted her eyes for a moment, lost in a fresh memory burning pain into the creases of her face, then refocused on Mom's face. "The men were talking about splitting up some of the women, trading them to other camps or groups for supplies." She bit her lip, peeked at me, then focused on her lap. "They mentioned your daughter."

Mom jerked back like she'd been slapped. "We just got here. Charlie promis—"

Angrily, Jeanine wrapped her fingers into Mom's jacket. "Charlie, huh? You think he's so great? He led the *activity* last night. And he was the one who brought her name up." She paused, her chest heaving with each impassioned gasp. "Did you know this was going to happen?"

Slowly shaking her head, Mom whispered. "No. I never would've come."

Searching Mom's face then mine, Jeanine drew back her lips in a snarl. "Leave. You have to. Before…" She looked down at herself as if realizing she had survived the incident. Sobbing, she tried covering herself up – even though she was fully clothed. "They're going to keep doing it. Over and over. They promised." Her entire body shook with spastic jerks.

Mom reached forward and wrapped her arms around Jeanine. The tight hold calmed the woman and Mom rocked her for a minute, maybe two. After Jeanine calmed down, Mom pulled back and met her gaze. "If we go, you're going with us. Do you think any of the other women would want to go?"

"You would want me to go with you?" Hope sparked behind the despair in Jeanine's eyes and the deep lines around her mouth and lining her forehead smoothed as she watched us for a trick or a lie.

"Of course. If we're getting out, you are, too." Mom stood, offering her hand to Jeanine and pulling her upright. "We need a plan. Other than meal times, what kind of a schedule are we looking at?"

"We haven't been here long enough for one to be implemented. Charlie kept the meal schedule because he didn't want to have so many people eating together. Mostly the perimeter watch is where the change is. He doesn't have everyone watching, only certain guys and they aren't from our original group. Our last chance will be by tomorrow morning. The perimeter is getting sealed so that the only things going in or out are by the front gate and with his permission." Her lip curved wistfully. "If only our plans would've worked out. We had some great things going, you know?"

"Still do, don't give up. We need to get out of here. Finding something else won't be hard." Mom slung her arm over my shoulder and pinned me to her side. Drawing Jeanine closer with a tug on her wrist, Mom lowered her voice. "Get your stuff together and we'll meet you tonight behind this building. When Kelly and I walked earlier, I noticed a small man-gate in the fence."

"I didn't see that, really?" How had I missed it? Oh, maybe that was when I had focused so hard on trying to convince Mom to leave. She'd been more aware of her surroundings than I assumed.

Jeanine pushed at the hair slipping from her rubber band and falling around her face. "Yeah, but it's guarded."

"We'll get around the guard. I'm not worried. Meet us right at dark and if you're there before us, wait outside the fence in the forest. We'll find each other." She met each of our gazes. "Don't wait inside, do you hear me? Just get out. Things are safer outside than in."

The camp had finally hit the horror point of being worse than the end of the world. How was Mom handling the breakdown of her plans?

The only way she knew how – make new ones.

B. R. PAULSON

CHAPTER 12

We skipped breakfast.

Returning to the hallway for our things, I couldn't help but try to look in the office for the dead guy again. But the door was shut tight. Snooping around the place hadn't been mentioned in our plans anyway. I needed to keep my focus. Not deviate.

Shaking off the death of a man I'd never met, I followed Mom down the hall.

My stomach growled, returning me to my previous thoughts. Back at the door to the pit we called our room for the time being, I shook my head and muttered, mostly to myself. "I can't believe we missed breakfast. Aren't you hungry?"

Mom pushed open the door and stopped abruptly. I smacked into her back. No, I wasn't paying attention because I had missed breakfast! "We have better food in our bags, Kelly." Which was probably true, if they only served oatmeal in the dining area. Not that they were allowing women to eat. I remembered where we would be eating and the prospect dimmed my hunger.

Craning my neck to see around her and why we stopped, I stared at the full visual of the mattress leaning against the wall, the one blanket strewn about the floor and mingling with the contents of our bags all over. We entered gingerly, closing the door behind us.

Clothes mingled with mashed in sandwiches flung from their baggies. Our MREs and other snack items seeped from split seams of their packages. I stood in the middle of the massacre and stared with my jaw thrust to the side.

Stepping over our things, Mom crossed to the closet and turned to look inside. Reaching up, she pulled the handgun from its hiding spot. Looking around, she took in the mess.

Resolve pressed her lips into a thin line. She motioned me closer, speaking so quietly like she breathed the words. "They don't trust us and they want us to know it. Let's get this cleaned up and get everything repacked. We don't have a lot of time." She patted my back and ducked down, already moving past the fact someone had dug through our things, throwing them all over the place.

How did she get over the invaded feeling? But as I lowered myself to the ground and crawled over our things, the truth hit me. She probably hadn't recovered from Charlie's invasion the night before. The looting of our room paled when compared to that event.

Could she forgive those trespasses against her? Or had Charlie taken her ability to practice her faith when he stole her Bible?

~~~

Our bags fully packed, the gun returned to its rightful pocket, Mom and I slouched on the edge of the bed.

A scratch on the back of her hand caught my eye. "Where'd you get that from?" The red line wasn't even deep enough to bleed, but I needed to talk. To hear the comfort of her voice. We'd been quiet for almost an hour while we worked.

She inspected the minor wound. "Hmm. I'm not sure." We didn't talk about the round circular bruises on her mid-forearm. As time passed more of Charlie's marks became visible, cementing the need to escape.

I entwined my fingers in my lap, studying them. No matter how long we lived, I would never be able to repay Mom for her sacrifices. She hadn't been protecting my virginity, but more saving me from being brutally raped and beaten. Hers and Jeanine's injuries proved so much worse than sex happened at the end.

"Do you think we're going to be okay?" Where had the tremor in my voice come from? I mastered the art of sounding like a scared twelve-year-old and I hadn't even been trying.

Mom shrugged, sliding to the ground and turning to face the bed. She folded her hands and bowed her head. "Let's pray. Whether we're okay or not, won't matter because we'll put our fate in His hands." She tucked her chin to her chest, not waiting for me to join her.

I stared at her, my lips partly open. I couldn't pray with her. I didn't want to. What would I pray about? I didn't have any gratitude for our position. I still hadn't made up my mind about the positive aspects of being alive considering everything we've gone through.

Mom prayed so easily. I envied her the ease to do something with assuredness.

Her prayer turned to a vigil.

Careful not to disturb her, I reached for the small pile of food left after the jerks had torn apart our supply. They hadn't even had the decency to eat the food, blatantly wasting resources in a time when stores weren't an option anymore.

Too much emptiness inside me needed filling. I couldn't wait. Before I knew what happened, a sandwich and a protein bar had disappeared. An aching sensation in my stomach was all I had left. But the emptiness hadn't diminished.

I gagged down the final bite of the bar. The thick protein bars weren't my favorite, but they landed like concrete in a never ending hole inside me. Eyeing the pile for more, I scratched at my stomach.

Mom lifted her head. I withdrew from the food, certain she would reprimand me for eating all our rations. But she didn't. She stood and moved to the door separating the bedrooms. Pushing her head to the panel, she listened for a moment.

Turning toward me, she crossed the short distance with a couple of long strides and bent down to whisper in my ear. "I need to get my Bible and the gun before we go."

Not "she wanted to," but "she needed to." Significant difference and one I wouldn't push aside. I nodded, eyes wide. "What can I do?" Who would I need to shoot?

Mom pulled back, pausing to search my face. "Really? You're not going to fight me?" Her bruises shamed me, but I forced myself to see them – see them for what they were.

Drawing my eyebrows together, I shook my head. "We don't have anything left to do before we go and you said *need.* If you *need* them, let's get them." Why the philosophy behind my agreement brought tears to her eyes, I'll never know. But there they were. I shifted to put my hands under my thighs.

"I'm not sure if Jeanine is getting ready or not. I'm not even sure if she's going to come with us, but we need all the fire power we can get, or I would leave the gun." She sat down beside me and looked at the floor. "If Braden and Dad's pictures weren't in the Bible, I might be fine leaving it, but since we need to get the gun anyway…"

Throwing my arm around her shoulders, I rested my chin on her arm. "So let's get the Bible, too. How do we do it?" I was willing but she had to come up with the plan.

She didn't need me to fight her. What she needed included me working with her so she didn't feel so alone.

I understood alone.

And I didn't like it.

~~~

Mom nudged my shoulder. She didn't whisper exactly, but in the quiet of the room, she could have and it would've been easy to hear. "Kelly, time to wake up. We need to go."

When had I fallen asleep? I picked my head up from my arms braced on my knees. I didn't remember sliding to the ground to sit. The last few hours blurred in my mind, melding together to create a confusing mish mash of realities.

We'd seen more than our share of horror movies and what happens when people split up. Self-quarantined in the room, Mom and I hadn't even gone to the bathroom except to use the toilet – which didn't work – in the adjoining bathroom.

But now it was time to put our plan into action and hope for the best. Or in Mom's case, hope your prayers did something.

I grimaced and pushed myself to stand. "How long did I sleep?" The afternoon light had dimmed. I blinked in the darkening room.

"About an hour." Mom rolled her head to one side and the other.

"Did you sleep?" I pulled my shoulders back to stretch them, tight from sleeping in a sitting position.

"No. I've been praying." Matter-of-factly, she didn't show any embarrassment. Why should she? I knew her beliefs, her faith. We planned to risk our lives for a book about her faith for crying out loud.

Of course, I grasped its importance. Even a hardcore atheist would understand – which I wasn't. I just didn't know that I could've prayed for an hour. Or a minute.

I nodded. What would I say? Sounds uncomfortable? Mom did most things old school and prayed as much as possible on her knees. I can't imagine she would shift to sitting or anything less than kneeling for even an hour straight of monologue with the Almighty.

For some reason, we hadn't discussed the reasons behind the co-op morphing into some kind of trafficking operation after only a couple of days. Or that they wanted to sell *me* pretty quick. "Why do you think Charlie is willing to get rid of me after he promised you he'd protect us?" I tugged my hair back into a manageable ponytail, off my neck and face. Plus, didn't he consider Mom *paid up* or anything after the night before?

Mom shrugged, twisting her own hair into a bun and drawing on her pack. "Do you think he's the type of guy to keep his word? I only agreed because I needed to buy us some time. But I was thinking more like months or weeks instead of hours." She offered me a small smile. "I'm sorry things didn't work out here. I really hoped they would."

"You're okay, Mom. I'm sorry it didn't work out here." For so many reasons I felt bad about the camp's failure. She invested a lot of her personal time and money toward the future the group had advertised. Because she hadn't planned on a power coup didn't mean her intentions sucked. Pulling on my pack, I welcomed the sturdy weight against my lower back and the tug on my shoulders. Something secure in the solidness of a plan.

She sighed. "You're disappointed."

"No, I'm not. At least not in you. In the group, yes, but you couldn't help the craziness." I arched my eyebrow. "Can you imagine if you had the kind of power to control all this? You could go and solve this entire crapshoot and we'd be able to go home." The longing for home reared its ugly head and engulfed me, bringing tears to my eyes.

Mom reached for me, drawing me close. "It's okay. I know this isn't ideal. None of this is even fun, but we're getting out. We'll survive. Remember the rules."

"Is that our mantra? 'Cause I think we could come up with something better." Anything would be better than *Stay alive, trust no one, and pray*. "Like, pee in someone else's yard, or something?"

Her laugh burst from her in a shocked gasp. "Kelly, you're so weird." But her smile softened the angry edges of the bruises on her face and the seemingly permanent sadness in the tilt of her lips.

I grinned back. We hadn't laughed together in so long. Usually our memories tied together in Dad and Braden. Their loss was just... sad. If we weren't reminiscing, we talked about survival. How to survive. What to do when. When and where and why and who. Everything was about surviving, like we forgot how to live.

Our gazes met and held. For a moment we basked in each other's company. As many problems as we had I wouldn't choose anyone else to go with me to the end of the world.

A scratching sounded at the doorway. Sitting benignly on the floor, like a small white rug, a scrap of paper had been shoved under the door. Mom claimed it, opening the folded piece to read its message.

The blood drained from her face. Her pallor more noticeable against the backdrop of her mahogany colored hair. She faced the window, the light beginning to dim.

"What? What's wrong?" Our situation crashed around us, banishing all humor from the room. We were back to survival.

"Jeanine says we have to do it now. They're coming for you at dark." Shoving the note into her front pocket, Mom twisted the door handle to Charlie's room. She didn't knock. Nothing. "He's locked it." She checked the window again.

The trees had turned to shadows against a darkening sky. A small amount of light kept everything from blending together, but not by much and not for long.

"Let's leave them." Mom turned toward the hall, sadness and worry warring for room on her face.

I grabbed her pack. "No. Mom, we need those. Come on." I pushed around her, opening our door and turning toward Charlie's room from the hall. Emboldened by the complex yet simplistic nature of our escape and the fact that I honestly didn't think we were going to be stopped, I turned the handle to his door and shoved my shoulder against the light wood.

My extra physical roughness wasn't necessary. The panel swung open easily and I stumbled inside, my momentum thrown off by the unexpected give.

Mom followed me inside, shutting the door behind us. She faced me, then glanced over my shoulder. Her eyes grew round and she spun me, grabbing the bottom panel of my backpack and yanking out the gun. The movement so fast, she had the gun out and aimed at Charlie before I even registered he had frozen in a half-standing, half-bending over position to pull on his pants.

Opening and closing, my mouth waited for direction from me that wasn't coming. I'm not completely sure where my confidence disappeared to, but if I found it, I would do something fearsome.

Charlie's smug grin pinched at the sides of his eyes, giving them a half-slanted appearance. He finished pulling up his pants and fastening them shut. Thank goodness. He tucked in the hem of his flannel and wiggled his eyebrow at Mom. "Are you bringing your daughter in for the fun tonight, Megan? I'm not gonna lie, I've been interested in you for a while now. Making this a mother-daughter event is very intriguing."

"Shut up. We're here for our things." Mom pushed me to the side, holding the gun steady at shoulder height. Got to hand it to her, she didn't shake when she held the weapon aimed on a man.

He nodded slightly toward her weapon. "I see you're not as forthcoming as your faith would demand."

"You don't know a thing about my faith or beliefs. Where's my stuff?" Mom's shoulders tightened more as she clenched the gun harder. "I have no problem shooting you, Charlie. After last night? Well, let's just say I'm looking for anything to pull this trigger."

Something on Mom's face must have testified to the truth because Charlie's humor vanished and something resembling fear and anger darkened his expression. "Where do you think you'll go? Huh? I run this place. You're not leaving unless I say." He stepped forward, his finger thrusting into the air between them.

"Take one more step. Please." Mom's silky, challenging tone sent chills to my toes. I never pushed her so far she stopped yelling or stopped talking normally. Her low dulcet tone… oh, I couldn't even imagine how much anger she tamped down.

He glanced to the side and back at Mom, staring her down. Mom didn't flinch. Charlie laughed, throwing his head back in so calculated a way, as if he tried holding our attention or changing our focus.

Following where he had looked, I searched the corner. A dresser and a lamp stood together. The empty top of the dresser seemed out of place in a man's bedroom. I crossed to the chest of drawers and pulled open the top.

Charlie stopped laughing. "Hey, you can't touch my things."

Mom's voice sharpened behind me. "Shut up."

Digging through the contents, I gripped the edges of Mom's Bible and waved the fluttering pages in the air. A small picture frame, silver and gold two-tone glinted in the corner under a leather-banded wristwatch. Jeanine sat in the photo with two boys about eight and twelve and a little girl around six. A handsome man draped his arm around her and the children and smiled with pride at the camera.

I added the photo to my collection.

The next drawer held our gun. Among other handguns and some extra ammo. "Mom, he has more ammunition in here." We could take it all, but we'd have a hard time carrying it.

"Good, grab out any that say .9 mm. We can take that with us." She didn't join me and I'm certain she wanted to, but she had to keep an eye on the bastard who wanted to trade me for toilet paper or whatever.

I tucked the orange and black boxes of rounds into my jacket pockets, as many as I could hold which left only two more boxes of the .9 mm caliber in the drawer.

"What did I say?" Mom's mild shriek made me spin. Charlie had advanced another step and smirked at her like he knew she was bluffing about shooting.

Something in his expression pushed Mom over the edge. She pulled the trigger, the crack sounding through the room like a clap of thunder.

Charlie's eyes jerked wide and he toppled backward, landing in a half-slump in the wing-backed chair. Blood brightened the upper sleeve of his arm. He moaned. At least he hadn't fallen on the bed.

Watching someone get shot was a heckuva lot easier than doing the actual shooting.

Mom faced me, gun still trained on the barely-clipped man. "We need to go. I'm betting that shot tipped our hand."

I tucked Jeanine's frame into an inside pocket of my jacket. Hopefully, I had a chance to give the photo to her. Hopefully, I didn't die in the next few minutes.

Better yet? Hopefully, I woke up and had breakfast with Dad and Braden in our old home because I didn't want to run again.

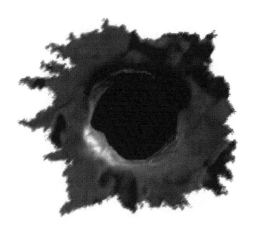

CHAPTER 13

Mom backed up to the doorway.

"Wait. We can't leave him like that. He's barely injured." I searched the dresser drawers. He had to have something I could use to immobilize him better. The third drawer down had an overabundance of duct tape and scissors. The details for such a large amount of tools were better left unknown. I yanked a full roll out and tore at the end.

Wrapping the silver tape around him and the chair, I did several passes around his torso, arms, and down around his legs to encompass the chair legs and back. I pulled his hand down from the wound and taped his hand down by his side.

He whimpered. "I need to stop the bleeding."

"You shouldn't have gotten shot, if you were worried about bleeding." I shrugged, ripping off the tape and patting the end in place. Stepping back, I admired my handiwork. "I could put more on his shoulders."

"That's good, Kelly. Come on." Mom checked out the door, holding the gun on me and Charlie.

Charlie's face paled. He shot a glance between Mom and I. "You're not going to leave me like this, are you?"

"Nope." I ripped off one more piece of wide tape and flattened the strip securely over his mouth. He turned his face but not before I had the external gag where I wanted. "I'm leaving you like *that*. You should've left my mom alone." I tossed the almost-gone tape roll on the desk and grabbed two more on our way out. Shutting the door to his room, we slowed our movements.

Who would be in the house at that time of day? We hadn't been in the camp long enough to get a solid idea of the schedule. The camp hadn't even been active long enough to sufficiently establish a set pattern either, but Charlie liked control. For him to establish certain times when "visiting" the main house was okay and not okay would not be out of character.

Halfway down the hall, we paused, trying to catch our racing nerves. My heart could've bumped right out of my chest. Mom shoved her hand against my stomach, looking forward.

Footsteps thundered up the deck stairs. The front door slammed open.

Mom jerked her head side to side, searching. I held my breath. What if we were caught? Fear shot through me. Mom and I would be separated. I might never see her again.

She pulled us forward, pushing open the first door to the right and shoving me inside. She followed, softly closing the door.

A different version of fear welled within me. I didn't want to turn around. I'd seen inside *that* room before. The buzz of the flies and the coppery scent of spilled blood would've been enough to warn me off. An all-new stench threatened me with stomach-curling acidity. Wrinkling my nose, I pressed my upper lip toward my nostrils but that didn't help.

Eyes watering, Mom looked over my shoulder. She closed her eyes. "Of course." She sighed and leaned her head against the wall. Pinching her nose and breathing through her mouth, she murmured. "I would pick this room."

Stomping from outside the door made us freeze. A fine sheen of sweat broke out over my body, even my toes felt damp. I reached for my mom's hand and squeezed her fingers when we connected.

She looked at me, offering a soft smile and nodding.

A shout from Charlie's room jerked us straighter under the weight of our bags. My shoulders ached from the continuous tension or the scent of death eating away at my body. Oh my word, I would've rather been caged with a skunk.

Waiting, wondering what was happening on the other side of the door, didn't make me more confident about our plan. The burns on my forearms itched and I loosely scratched at them.

Mom knocked my hand away. She hated when I did that to any scab or other wound, something about causing an infection. She held her finger to her lips.

She closed her eyes, mouth moving enough to suggest she prayed. I too closed my eyes and asked – somebody, anybody – to keep us safe.

Charlie's bellows joined the voices of the men who rescued him. "They're trying to steal from us. Get them." Great, branded as thieves, we would never get out alive, if not safe and sound – if people saw us anyway.

The men stormed down the hall toward the front door. I hadn't released Mom's hand and clung as they passed. We breathed a little easier when the thunderous band slammed the front door.

A boot fall from the direction of Charlie's room cooled our relief. A door on the opposite side of the hallway opened carefully and closed after a drawn out forty-five seconds or so. The next door was treated the same way.

Then the door next to us.

Our eyes met and Mom pointed toward the corner behind the door. We tiptoed as well as we could with the heavy packs on our backs and squished against the wall, tucked in like sardines. Mom lifted the barrel of the gun to run parallel with her face and directed toward the ceiling.

I sucked in my stomach. Hmm, to make myself skinnier and try to help me hide better? As ineffective as it was. At least the action decreased my inadequacy because I was doing *something*.

The door handle turned right in front of us – like a horrible movie from long ago. I bit my lip to keep from crying out.

We stopped moving, not even blinking. Solid walls behind me and to the side of me added to the claustrophobia of the moment and I panted, the barest amount with hardly any sound.

Opening, the panel stopped an inch from our faces, completely blocking us from view of anyone in the room. The man grunted and shut the door, probably deterred from his search by the stench of the rotting corpse.

Yeah, buddy, I couldn't agree more.

His footsteps moved further down the hall but the front door didn't open or close.

Mom's whisper barely carried across the space separating us. "We're going to go out the window. I'm not sure he's gone." She moved to the window and pushed at the double-glass vinyl pane, lifting it soundlessly from its setting.

Sticking her head out the hole, she turned left and right, taking in the surroundings. Fortunately, this side of the house also faced a viewless scene of fence, dirt, and grass with trees in the background. She didn't come back inside, but rather climbed over the low windowsill.

Crouching outside the opening, she motioned me forward. The encouragement wasn't necessary. I couldn't be more anxious to escape that odorous hellhole. The fresh breeze from the window provided too sweet a possible escape.

I fell through, landing on the veranda with an oomph.

Mom reached for me, but not to help. She covered my mouth with her hand and shook her head. Eyes searching around us, she barely moved as she took in our surroundings. She shifted her hand from my lips to under my arm and pulled me up.

Shouting carried from the front of the house and we backed against the log siding. I tried slowing my inhales and exhales.

"What are we going to do?" My chest tightened as I whispered and I struggled against the fear every yell flooded through me.

Mom didn't answer. Instead, she pushed me toward the back of the house, away from noises. The dark covered us enough even if someone had looked down the veranda, they probably would've only seen shadows. Hopefully, anyway.

We pushed outward toward the fence, holding close to the solid line as we ran the perimeter. How could the men not see us? When I gathered enough courage to check for pursuers or someone who might spot us, I couldn't find anyone. The only person in view was Mom.

We passed the latrine, the dining area, and suddenly Mom stopped the frantic half-crouch-run we'd both fallen into. I grabbed her backpack as I slowed to avoid crashing headlong into her.

She peeked around the corner of the back exit. The gate had been left open a few inches. A memory of our dead dog decided to resurface and I grimaced. Open gates didn't have a good history with me.

From our new vantage point, the entrance to the compound – the way we entered anyway before – received more attention than where we were. Men milled about while a generator-powered set of flood lights lit up the clearing. Our position fell about eight feet outside the sea of light.

"Psst. Megan, over here." Jeanine's frantic whisper reached us from the woods.

Mom pushed the door open enough we could slip out and she all but shoved me through. Closing the gate carefully behind us, she continued pushing at me like I wasn't moving fast enough, even as we sprinted across the dirt path between the fence and the forest line.

As we reached her, Jeanine clutched Mom's hands, pulling her into a short embrace. "I didn't think you guys were coming."

Mom shook her head. "We got caught up in the house. I shot Charlie."

Jaw dropping, Jeanine stared at Mom. "What? Is he dead? The bastard."

"No, but the shot drew attention to us. I wouldn't be surprised if they chase after us, now." Mom ducked further into the woods. "Come on, we need to get those rifles."

I forgot about the guns.

Like on autopilot I followed Mom and Jeanine deeper into the darkness, deeper into the clutching branches and roots trying to trip us. The two women slowed down the further we went.

"We're almost there, let's rest here for a second. Kelly, you okay?" Mom bent at the waist, her pack riding up her back until she stood again. "Jeanine, you good?"

"I'm sore, but I'll be fine." Jeanine's expression hid in the shadows, but her increasing limp could be seen even without light.

We fell silent, taking another moment to reclaim our bearings.

The snap of a twig sent my heart to racing again. Mom and Jeanine glanced at each other. Mom lowered her voice to a whisper. "We need to go."

How? Did we run and give the people chasing us a direction? Or did we walk as quietly as possible and hope we moved fast enough to evade whoever followed us in the woods?

We broke into a run and the clouds parted. Moonlight revealed our route like a flip had been switched. My pack bounced into my upper hips and lower back with each step. At least my tightly bound chest benefited me more than bugged me.

We came upon the clearing quickly, passing through to the other side where Mom and I had first spotted Jeanine. Out of the clearing, Jeanine and I stood guard along the edge while Mom searched for the guns left behind. The ones we stole from Shane and his injured friend what felt like eons ago but was only days.

Days.

The world had ended days ago and the craziness I jumped into with my mother got worse by the minute.

Jeanine slapped my arm and pointed into the clearing. A man, a guard I recognized from breakfast, stepped into the open. His eyes hidden by the hulking mass of his eyebrows, he searched for us. Who else would he be looking for?

A shout from behind him pulled his attention and he turned.

Jeanine raised her hand, a pistol in her fingers. She aimed and pulled the trigger.

Everything happened too fast for me to do anything but react. I dropped to the ground, certain a huge gun fight would zing bullets around me any moment.

The man fell to the ground, his own gun flashing in the white moonlight. The crack of the second shot mingled with the first as the sound faded into silence.

All hell broke loose as men shouting and yelling surrounded our position.

"Over here. They must be this way. Come on."

"Get the girls. Don't kill them."

"Those stupid women. We're going to get you!"

I Army-crawled backwards toward Mom. Whispering, I nudged Jeanine's foot. "Come on, get down."

She held her stance, gun in front of her, ready to blaze away. "Find your mom and get out of here. I'll hold them off."

I stood because I wasn't getting anywhere on my stupid stomach and my pack threatened to suffocate me, pressing on my chest in the dirt.

Mom was only a few feet back, slinging the rifles to her shoulders. "Jeanine, this way." Her whisper must have carried to the woman because Jeanine turned and ran after us in her limping cadence. Mom led us through a thick tangle of brush which was surprisingly quiet compared to the way we came in.

We could make it to the road— maybe. Did we want to, though? Even a non-strategist like myself understood watching the road would be a simple task for the men.

Either way, I didn't care. I wanted out of those woods. Out of the game.

Who said survival was important anyway?

CHAPTER 14

Gravel crunched under our boots, the sound unexpectedly shocking when we had grown used to soft footfalls on padded forest floor.

"We made it to the road. Let's keep going north and stay away from the neighborhoods." Mom angled northeast and stepped off the road, to walk in the ditch. "Jeanine, did you hear anything about how the towns are doing? Has the fighting stopped?"

"There isn't much left of anything to fight. I heard the president and his cabinet are all gone, but no one is sure. Oh, and a rumor that California was nuked by Russia." Jeanine fell into step beside Mom but she stayed on the road. The ditch could have been too much for her limp. I didn't want to ask why she limped. The suggestion of what those men had done to her gave me enough pause to respect what privacy she had left.

"Which part of California?" Mom's voice didn't carry far, but reached me as I followed silently behind them.

This was their moment to catch up, find some kind of control. I didn't have any questions anyway. The people I cared about were gone. All except for Mom.

Gravel glinted in the moonlight. Something about the serenity of the moment lulled me into a cadence. We stopped listening to everything around us and focused on us.

"All of it. Seriously, from what I understood, the fallout carried into Nevada and southern Oregon. So much land wasted." Jeanine's mocking laugh cut off with the retort of a rifle from the distance. Judging from the pop, the caliber couldn't be larger than a .22 but who would carry a rodent gun in a situation during the end of the world?

I fell to the side, landing in a prickly collection of weeds, scratching my bare hands and leaving stickers in my pants. Jeanine dropped into a crouch, shooting at the dark shadow about twenty feet behind us. How had we missed him? He got so close.

Four shots from Jeanine and he fell to the ground.

Where was Mom?

"Megan? Where are you?" Jeanine crawled down the dip in the ditch and searched around the spot where Mom had stood.

I rushed to my feet, brushing at the stickers on my jeans.

"Get down, Kelly." Jeanine whispered at me, waving her arms. "We don't know how many more are out there."

Mom groaned. "Kelly, down." Her voice directed us toward a collection of Aspen trees.

Jeanine and I pushed through the brush to get to Mom.

She had pushed herself against a tree, leaning on her pack, holding her gun at the ready. She met my gaze, eyes wet. "I'm fine. We need to get out of here." Over my shoulder, to Jeanine she asked. "Do you know of any houses up this way we could hide in?"

Jeanine shook her head, cradling her arm which had started bleeding. "This isn't my area. My family… we lived in Post Falls. Rathdrum and Athol, this is all way too far north for me."

"Jeanine, you're bleeding." I pointed at her upper arm.

She glanced down and stared for a moment. Shrugging, she moved her arm. "It's not a big deal. Doesn't feel like it's too bad."

"We need to move, Jeanine. We don't know when the next one will be here." She gasped. She closed her eyes and leaned her head against the tree for a brief moment.

"Mom, what's wrong?" Had she been hit? Why would she hide it? My mom wouldn't get hit by something as mundane as a .22 caliber shot. Would she?

"I… I think he shot me." She laughed, more at herself than with humor.

"Where?" Jeanine cradled her arm, pushing against the bleeding wound.

"Stomach?" Mom inhaled and tried keeping her hand on her side. "It doesn't feel like a big hole or anything, but I can tell I've been hit." She coughed, but not before a whimper escaped her lips.

Jeanine slumped into her crouch. "Stomach? Megan…"

"Shh. I know. Can we do something to get out of sight? At least for a bit? We need some time to figure out what to do." She searched Jeanine's face, desperation rich in the lines by her mouth and eyes.

"Let me think." Jeanine stared into the blackness of the forest.

I couldn't breathe. What was happening? How could Mom get shot in the stomach? "It's not that serious, right, Mom?" A gut shot had a specific meaning when hunting, but it couldn't be the same for humans. We would take her to the hospital... they'd... fix...

My eyes met hers, dark and knowing as it dawned on me there wasn't anyone at the hospitals anymore to help us. So she'd been shot. In the stomach. A gut shot my dad used to call them. Even a .22 could do irreparable damage when there was no way to treat the wound. Even with a nurse on hand to give instructions.

Nausea overcame me and I turned my head, bent over, and vomited what contents I'd had in my stomach. I'm not normally quiet when I throw up, but I didn't really have any other options in the dark of the night with men chasing us – shooting us.

Jeanine snapped her fingers, the click redirecting my attention. Of course she was right, I needed to focus. I wiped my mouth. What could I do? Something, not nothing. I could help my mom. Mom was invincible and something as lame as a bullet would never bring her down. Both women ignored my display. I acted like it hadn't happened.

"Can you walk, Megan?" Jeanine didn't lower her hand, fingers held tight to her palm.

Mom shook her head. Jeanine nodded. "Kelly, you'll stay here and I'll check the nearby houses for a wheelbarrow or something we can move your mom in." Jeanine ducked out from under the branches and disappeared before I could stop her, ask her what we were going to do.

I couldn't look my mom in the eye. Patting her shoulder, I watched for movement or anything else that could be dangerous. "Are you okay, Mom? Keep pressure on it."

She coughed into a soft chuckle. "I'm the nurse. I know how to stop bleeding." She clutched her fist to her side, like she had an ache which wouldn't go away. Sadly, that's exactly what she had.

We waited for what seemed like forever. Any type of sound shot my heart rate through the roof and my breathing cut into panting. Mom reached for my hand and I gripped hers like the last bottle of water in the desert.

The moon moved higher in the sky and men's voices called off in the distance, their echo low in the dark. But, thankfully, they grew fainter and fainter. My chest moved easier and my grip lessened on her fingers. "Mom, I think we're going to be —"

Crashing and gravel crunching cut me off and I moved in front of Mom, dropping her hand.

Where had they come from? I was prepared to take the next bullet for her.

"Shh." Mom pushed the air through her teeth with little effort, the hiss barely discernible.

If I could scream, I would, but my voice had disappeared.

"Megan? Kelly?" Jeanine's whisper sent a rush of relief through me. The men weren't crashing toward us, coming to trade me off and hurt my mom.

"Here. We're here." I stood, looking for her on the road.

She came into view, pulling a gardening wagon behind her – bigger than a child's with large pneumatic wheels. "Let's get your mom loaded. Come on."

I reached down for Mom and helped her up, taking as much of her weight as she would let me. Which wasn't much because her stubbornness could challenge concrete.

She limped the few feet down the ditch and up to the gravel shoulder. Hunched over into an almost standing-fetal position, she collapsed over the side of the wagon. The corner of the metal side snagged her jacket.

"Grab your packs, Kelly. We don't have time to do anything else." Jeanine adjusted Mom's legs and arms, turning her fuller onto her back. She spoke to Mom. "Keep your hand on your stomach, Megan. We might be able to find some place with first aid supplies." She lifted her gaze, watching me as I gaped at my mom's inert figure. "Go, *now*, Kelly."

The packs. I stumbled backwards, tripping over my own feet. We left the packs by the trees. I grabbed them, faltering under their weight. I hadn't slept in so long, fatigue, worry, and the stress of the last few days added up, pulling at my shoulders and back.

When would this end?

Would it?

Time for a break. The world needed to stop the craziness and open up hospitals. My mom needed help. We needed help. What could I do to make it all go away?

How could I fix this?

Could I?

Or was I going to be forced to watch my mom die?

Under the weight of the packs, I crawled up the side of the ditch and swung Mom's over the side of the wagon. Pulling my straps on right, I shimmied my pack into the correct position and checked the road behind us and in front of us. Weird, usually my mom was the cautious one and I was oblivious.

"I'm going to need your help pulling this. My arm isn't quite right and I had a hard time with it empty." Jeanine raised her left arm, the fingers and lower forearm stained with dark streaks tracing from her wound. Thankfully the full extent of her injuries weren't clear in the dark.

The small mercies, I guess. How much could I cope with? My limit had to be around there somewhere.

She clutched at the flesh above the dark red hole in her arm and twisted her lips.

"You need to keep pressure on that. I'll pull my mom." I learned a lot with a mother for a nurse. I wasn't as knowledgeable as her, but I helped in emergencies growing up and I could stitch a thing or two. Okay, so not really. I watched her do stitches and deliver a baby as well as help with a few other things, so I understood the theories. The most common thing I always heard growing up was 'put pressure on it'.

When I started my period, I worried I needed to put pressure on *it*. Not something you want to do at twelve. I asked Mom about it and she had laughed so hard, Dad had run in the room to see if she was alright. They both laughed for a few days afterwards. I don't remember anything funny about my question.

I took the long handle to the wagon and dug my feet into the rocky road, pushing my weight forward. The larger tires moved surprisingly well and didn't take as much energy or strength as I expected.

Mom groaned, the sound more alarming since I hadn't heard anything from her since we put her in the cart. "Everything okay?" I glanced at Jeanine. She trundled along beside us, eyes focused down as she clutched her arm.

Crap, I was the only one left uninjured. What did that mean? *Oh, please, please, let them be okay. Please. We need a safe place to hide. Please.* I picked up my pace, scanning the trees for something, anything.

But my plea must have fallen on deaf ears.

A shot rang out, zinging into the rocks off to our left, but not by much.

I sobbed. Seriously, how much more did we have to take? I hadn't been shot yet, would this macabre game go until all three of us bled from a hole in our bodies?

Pulling harder, I broke into a trot, the wagon following me easily. My pack dragged at me and I forced my sobs down and quieted my crying. Tears wouldn't get us out of there.

Jeanine turned, shooting behind us at nothing in particular. The light wasn't enough to see into the forest line. We were easier to see because we had nothing to hide behind on the gravel.

"We need to get off this road." How long had we been walking? I didn't even know where we were. A Y in the road loomed and I pulled to the right. We needed to get out of the line of sight so we could disappear from view.

Another shot and a shout from behind us. Judging from the faintness of the call, they were far enough behind us we had a small window of time to try and hide. I dug in harder, harder still. Jeanine panted as she kept up with me. I ignored the small whimpers coming from Mom. If I focused on her pain and discomfort, I wouldn't try so hard to get us out of there so fast.

We broke past the line of sight and trees muffled the noises coming from our pursuers. Walking a few more feet, I stopped. "Look, we're in a roundabout. We have too many options and no idea which way to go. Let's get up in the center island."

"The center? They'll find us." Jeanine watched the road behind us, her gaze spastic as she searched for the briefest glimpse of our followers.

"Not in the chunk of trees there. They'd never suspect we would hide with so many roads to choose from. Help me get the wagon up there and hide the tracks." I pulled hard, turning the front wheels and jerking the wagon behind me. We would make noise but if we moved fast, we could trim down the time and get silent before the men got within range.

Jeanine took up the rear. She pushed with her one good hand and helped me maneuver the cart up the sloping dirt, into the copse of trees and bush not torn out when the roundabout had been put in. I dropped back, straightening as much grass and roadside weed as possible. I dragged my foot back and forth over the tracks in the soft gravel on the side of the road.

Returning to the wagon, I helped Jeanine as she adjusted branches and leaves to cover the glossy paint of the wagon metal and Mom.

After we tucked ourselves as deep into the center of the natural camouflage as we could, I took a seat on the ground and leaned against the side of the wagon. I needed water and a nap. Pulling my canteen from my pack, I sipped carefully. The water hadn't even had time to grow stale since we'd abandoned our home a few days before. The taste reminiscent of home, so familiar and yet so foreign.

Turning, I checked Mom to see if she was awake to drink something, but her eyes were closed and she breathed erratically. I didn't want to wake her and possibly increase her discomfort.

I held up the canteen, noticing for the first time Jeanine didn't have any supplies with her besides a small fanny pack around her waist. I pushed at her leg and offered the canteen into the air.

She smiled, taking the water and sipping it, closing her eyes. Lowering the canteen, she wiped the back of her hand across her lips. "Thank you." She mouthed with no sound. She glanced between Mom and me and then gazed back the way we came, searching for something.

Once when I'd gone on a hunting trip with my dad, he pointed out only prey watched for danger. So the shining of their eyes gave their position away. He taught me to keep my eyes down, shielded and not to look directly toward anything or anybody when in the dark. I usually ruled at Evening Capture the Flag with my friends because of this.

Jeanine had obviously never been taught or she never would've watched the road behind us with abandon.

I reached into my pocket, determined to get her to look away from the road, hide her eyes. Pulling out the picture frame, I tugged at her pants again.

She glanced down to be courteous. But when her gaze landed on the frame, the glint of the metal and glass in the meager light, she froze. Slowly reaching for the picture, her fingers trembled and she gasped, the sound barely louder than a leave falling from a tree.

Tears glistened on her cheeks, and she became more than someone my mom knew.

This woman had children and a husband and for whatever reason, they weren't with her. She'd been damaged and destroyed and shot. Warmth filled my chest when I realized she was like us, her story and her value hadn't diminished because of the end.

More shouts carried to us, but closer. Jeanine didn't acknowledge them right away. She traced the small faces of her children with her forefinger, a soft smile playing on her lips. Glancing up at me, tears still bright on her cheeks and in her eyes, she whispered, "Thank you, Kelly. I needed this."

She leaned down and kissed Mom's forehead, whispering, "Megan, hang in there. Thank you." She nodded, holding her finger to her lips, her injured arm dangling at her side. "Don't do anything until daylight and you're sure no one's around." Then she disappeared.

A moment passed. Her footsteps crashed through the underbrush, scuffling when she reached the gravel.

Her uneven gait faded under the dry rasp of my panting.

An empty moment passed filled with the panic of my heart beats rushing in my ears.

Suddenly shouts and shots broke up the stillness of the night.

Indecipherable yelling reached me through the padding of trees and branches. I dug my fingers into the soft dirt and pressed my face into my knees.

Jeanine screamed, screamed, screamed, another shot and she…

Stopped.

My breathing caught.

Men whooping like Indians in a poorly made Cowboys and Indians film surrounded me from not too far off. I lifted my head and crossed my arms. Sadness and disbelief overwhelmed me.

She was gone.

Gone.

What the heck was I supposed to do with my mom? All by myself?

CHAPTER 15

The party over Jeanine's death faded minutes after starting. Like a sample of what was to come, the intensity of the search for Mom and I increased. Palpable, like a mist in the air, the hunt fever drenched the woods, soaking us.

Thankfully Mom didn't make any more noises. I'm not sure if this was a good thing or not from a medical standpoint. Coming from our position, her silence worked for the time being.

I turned to kneel beside the wagon, checking her wound for more bleeding. The blood didn't gush or even seep fast, but the dampness covered the area like it bled some here and there.

Setting my pack down, I used the bulk as a pillow. Pine needles and spring growth weren't my first choice as a bed, but I'd take what I could get. We weren't going to get very far in the dark, not with a frenzied hunting party after us or with Mom injured like she was.

I wrapped my arms around my waist, holding my stomach and staring into the black, star-speckled sky above me.

Boots stomped on gravel all around us, the startling nearness deafening and incapacitating.

The roundabout branched out in four different directions – the direction we came from, and three others. At least a dozen men paced and walked around the center island searching for a clue as to which way we had gone.

Nothing would move me from my spot. I could stare at the sky and no one would see the shine of my eyes.

Every time they called to each other, I flinched. Would they wake Mom? Would she make a sound? Fear enhanced selfish thoughts. I didn't want to die. I didn't want Mom to either. If she stayed asleep and quiet, our chances increased by the minute of surviving until morning.

What would they do if they did find us? Would they shoot us, like Jeanine? Or would they take us back and do worse things?

Included with our nightly instructions, Mom would always warn me about the good, better, best phenomenon which applied to even the bad, worse, worst alteration.

In theory, things worked like this: Events start out good/bad like someone gets a job or gets a cold. In the next step of better/worse that job would come with a huge salary and the cold would turn to pneumonia. In either situation, the person would be thinking "how could things get better or worse?" And then the best/worst would come like a promotion or bonus and death.

Before being able to go the other way on the spectrum, their circumstances had to go to the extreme of best/worst.

So even while lying with my mom shot and men chasing after us, I wasn't stupid enough to believe things would get better so soon. We still hadn't survived the worst.

I just didn't know what the worst could be.

Death? Or was surviving the worst and death would be the better?

Even as the men continued searching, I couldn't fight the pull on my eyelids anymore. I slept.

~~~

I'm not sure what woke me.

One second I was asleep and the next I wasn't. Rather than a gradual wakening, I blinked at the early morning light with a snap like a victim of hypnosis. Dew covered me and small droplets sparkled on my lashes, filling my vision with streaks of light.

Wiping my face partially dry with my damp sleeve, I shivered and sat up. We hadn't been discovered. Nothing outside of our small safety site suggested they searched nearby for us.

I turned toward Mom, her pale skin and shallow breathing didn't create warm fuzzies in my chest. Dread tightened around my ribs. She shivered.

Touching her arm, I whispered, "Mom? Which way should we go? I'll get us out of here, but I'm not sure where to take you."

She licked her lips, which didn't do much to moisten them, and breathed. "North."

North it would be. The roundabout had distinct north, south, east, and west roads coming in and going out. The sun had risen from the east so choosing the correct road wasn't difficult.

I continued glancing around, as I shrugged my jacket off. The moisture magnified the chill and did me less good on than I wanted. Kicking the concealing brush from the wagon, I longed to pee but no way would I waste another moment, waiting to be found. If we could get to a scene of relative safety, I'd be able to take care of Mom's wound as well as our basic needs.

"Hang on, things are going to be bumpy for a bit." I pulled on the handle, the wagon easily following me down the slight hill and onto the road. Glancing left and right continuously, I pulled the wagon, counting one-hundred steps. Then I stopped for a break.

Another one-hundred. A break.

On my third break, Mom's croaked question reached me. "Where's Jeanine?"

I shook my head, without looking back at her. I didn't want to wait for another part to the inquiry so I cut my break and pulled forward again. This time, I stretched myself to two-hundred steps, ignoring the burn in my thighs and lower back.

Five-hundred steps. Approximately five-hundred yards. I had no idea where I was going or even if I would... wait a minute, I recognized the mailbox feet from me. Camouflage paint covered the metal box and a deer antler protruded from the side as the flag.

I stared at the start of the driveway. The last time I had been in that spot, I'd volunteered to drop off track and cross country information for Bodey Christianson. Our track coach hadn't been able to get a hold of him and I wanted the chance to see him, talk to him for a second.

Not many opportunities to be around him when he was home-schooled. We didn't share classes so track meetings or math meets were highlights I looked forward to. I had sat in the car

I borrowed from Mom and stared at their mailbox, worried I was walking into a trap or something. What if his parents had been into some kind of trespassers-shot-on-sight kind of thing? My nerves had been present more then, than now.

Glancing behind us, I didn't think anymore. I pulled Mom up the windy, twisty driveway and crossed my fingers someone would be there to help.

On that day so long ago – okay months — when I came with my handful of pamphlets and my track sweat-suit on, a couple of golden Labradors had greeted me halfway up the driveway. The two friendly dogs hadn't hesitated in licking my hands and jumping to place their front paws on my thighs.

Where were they as I struggled to pull Mom up the slightly inclined drive? Why didn't they come loping out of the trees with their tongues hanging out, tails wagging like paper fluttering in the wind?

Moisture collected between my pressed-down breasts. I don't remember what a clean face felt like and I smelled bad – I could smell myself! I would never forgive myself, if Bodey saw me like that. But I'd never forgive myself *more*, if I wished them to be gone. Instead, I hoped they were there, watching from their windows for signs of people who may or may not be safe. I hoped they hunkered down, locking their dogs in the shop or garage to keep them from running off.

I rounded the curve of their looping driveway and took in the open curtains and empty garage – the front door to the house stood open. If they left, they wouldn't make it. They couldn't. Not when there wasn't any place left for people to be safe.

My sadness deepened at this latest loss. I hadn't wanted to accept so many were dying, disappearing, gone. Why did this last hope of mine have to be dashed so soon after the end? A sob tore through me and I caught it with a gasp, careful to keep my control, at least until I could get Mom inside and resting on a more comfortable surface. I could disappear into the woods and lose my sanity once I took care of Mom.

The nearness of protection gave me enough oomph to crest the final slight rise of the hill. At the plateau of the drive, I relaxed my shoulders and paused. For a moment. We weren't safe, not out in the open. Not where anyone could still get to us.

Did I go into the house? I didn't want to chance encountering dead bodies. I hadn't known Bodey's sister well, but the few times I'd seen her she smiled so nice.

The final thing to break me would be seeing the Christianson family torn apart in some way. Picturing them together and safe somewhere gave me the smallest sense of security. The smallest sense of... I don't know, hope Mom and I would be safe for a while.

Keeping my voice down, I faced my mom, who hadn't yet woken completely. "I'm going to see if I can get into the shop. We should be fine in there."

Her lips moved but I couldn't tell if she understood. Her eyelids didn't flicker.

Unwilling or unable to leave her in the middle of the drive, I pulled the wagon to the rear of the shop, where a man-door stood stalwart against intruders. The half-door glass window was covered resolutely in vertical blinds.

But I needed in. We needed in.

The handle didn't turn either way. Crap, nothing would be simple. I picked up a rock the size of my fist and turned my face away from the building. Slamming through the single pane didn't take as much energy as I used. The ease shocked me and I released the rock when I shoved it through the window. The solid thud when it landed inside made me squeeze my eyes shut. No idea why the glass tinkling and shattering didn't bother me half as much as the sound of the rock landing.

I waited. Counting. Five, six, seven... thirty, thirty-one... I blew out and inhaled, watching, waiting. Fifty, fifty-one... how high would I go? How long would I wait? Ninety-nine, one-hundred. If nobody had charged after me by then, I assumed they wouldn't.

Reaching inside, I unlocked the handle so I could twist it open from the outside. Pushing the panel open, I gingerly stepped over the shards of glass and into an apartment style entryway.

The doorway was wide enough I pulled the wagon through. Already the warmth in the shop intensified the coolness of my skin. When had the weather grown so cool? Or had I not warmed up from the previous night? I closed the mangled door.

The large shop had multiple wings and bays. Where we stood encapsulated a semblance of a kitchen and eating area, like an afterthought. Pulling Mom through the room, we entered another area set up with an ammunitions reloader and weapons storage. I'd never seen so many arrows in my life.

Hanging from the rafters, a full-sized canopy for a truck had been strung up alongside ladders, bins, and a tennis ball hanging from a string.

Some people could be weird, if they wanted to be. I arched my eyebrow and ducked around the neon green ball. A smaller man-door stood closed on the far side. I pulled Mom harder, over downed lumber and other tools randomly left out. The grating of metal on concrete wasn't pleasant on the ears.

The door gave easily and I looked cautiously inside what could only be described as extra storage. Random folded tarps rested on barrels of oil. Rolled up carpet had been stacked in the corner beside yards and yards of coiled extension cord.

Exposed insulation in the walls explained the warmth. Small windows along the top of the rear wall allowed light into the small area, but not too much. Pushing Mom inside the room, I closed the door on the wagon, careful to keep as much warmth as possible in the small space.

Shop blankets had been thrown into a haphazard pile, manning the tops of more barrels and buckets. I grabbed as many as I could and laid them out in the semblance of a bed.

Shaking my mom's shoulder, I spoke softly, but with enough firmness to make her respond. "Mom, you need to wake up and get out of the wagon. Can you help me? Mom?" Hold on a little longer and I could lose whatever I was holding on to. I could cry. But not yet. Not when Mom hung on with her fingernails.

After a long moment filled with me shaking her shoulders and murmuring direction, she stirred, pushing herself from the bed of the wagon to a semi-standing but more fetal position. She groaned.

"I'm sorry, I know you hurt. Here, let's get you over here. You can lie down." I draped her unused arm around my shoulders and pulled her to lean on me as much as she could. She wavered like someone pushed her back and forth on her feet. "You're okay, Mom. Come on. I'll help you get to the floor. Right here." She collapsed onto the makeshift bed.

Yanking our backpacks closer to where she dropped, I rummaged through their contents for a first-aid kit. "Mom, where'd our first-aid kits go?" But she'd already fallen asleep again. The packages couldn't have fallen out. Another thing stolen from us at camp. Shaking my head, I pushed items around in a search for something to eat. Anything.

A few packets of jerky fell out. "Where did our food go?" The jerks at the camp hadn't destroyed everything. We should have still had a few snacks left. Everything was gone but the jerky.

"Crap, crap, crap, crap." I banged the back of my head on the carpet rolls behind us and stared at the ceiling. "We need food and supplies.

Please, we need something to eat." I didn't want to pray, not out loud, but I was there – at the end of one of our trials and I needed food. For both me and Mom. We needed food. STAT.

Mom always exhorted praying as the best thing in the world, but I sat with her on the blanket for minutes, an hour, praying and praying for something to eat to fall from the sky. Or come inside and let us eat it. I wasn't being selfish. I wanted my mom to have something to eat. Something to help her get better. She *had* to get better.

I avoided her stomach. She had the skills and experience to look at the wound and she kept passing out. I understood, but if it's so bad she can't even see it? What was I supposed to do? I couldn't step in. My knowledge only took me so far and we already covered *put pressure on it*.

"Kelly." Mom licked her lips and motioned me closer. Her lowered voice didn't prepare me for her request. "I need you to look at the wound site and help me."

"But… Mom, I'm not… I'm not sure…" I swallowed. I loved her, and so I had to tell her I didn't like blood. So much about that moment freaked me out. I could handle blood, it was *her* blood I didn't want to see. Her weakness. All of the blood meant she didn't have it inside her – keeping her alive. I needed her alive.

"I know, baby girl." She paused to breathe, like she needed a break. Since when did my mother need a break when talking? "But you need to get used to it sooner or later, okay? This is… Good practice."

Squirming for another ten seconds, I finally bit the inside of my cheek and flared my nostrils. The scent of blood didn't strike me as particularly appealing, but the coppery odor was easier to take on an empty stomach than one full and ready to vomit its contents.

I lifted her shirt hem, pulling the line to her bra-line. The blood covered most of her lower abdomen, like she had been bleeding for a while and her stomach had been made from a spongey material. "Okay, I see it."

She had closed her eyes, but hadn't fallen asleep. "Wipe what blood you can away and look for an exit wound."

Exit wound? Seriously? I ground my teeth together, wincing at the painful tightness in my jaw but grateful for the distraction. I swiped the loose material of her shirt over the thick red blood, smearing it across her smooth skin.

Angling my neck, I inspected her other side, feeling more with my fingers than seeing. I didn't want to move her and searching with my hands didn't disturb me as much as visually searching would. I did *not* want to see more blood.

The smoothness of her back had me pursing my lips. "I don't feel anything. Looks like there isn't an exit?" I pulled back staring at the small hole, confused. "The hole looks bigger than a twenty-two, though."

She allowed a slit in her eyelid when she peeked at me. "What do you mean twenty-two?"

"The rifle that guy shot you with was a twenty-two, right? That's what it sounded like." I shrugged, offering a small reassuring smile – well, what I hoped was comforting. "Shouldn't be too deep, Mom. Might be able to do a finger search for it yourself." Satisfied with my diagnosis, I settled onto my haunches.

"No, the bullet was a forty-four. Jeanine's shots ricocheted. I was hit after I jumped into the woods. I couldn't make myself tell Jeanine… she would never forgive herself." Mom shook her head, swallowing, the effort obviously hard. "Since the bullet didn't go through me, it's in there and judging from the pain, it's in there good." She drew in a ragged breath.

What did I do? How did you say sorry for friendly fire? I only ever heard about the horror when we watched a movie from a long time ago my parents had saved from before the purge. A man had been shot while running from his family to his friends. With friendly fire. Dad had described it. I never heard of such a thing. They didn't teach things in history or the rest of school about much of anything.

A stack of blue paper towels was piled on the counter beside the door. I stood and grabbed all of them, returning to Mom to put some on her stomach like a bandage. Tugging her shirt back down, I stared at the lump of towels as if my glare alone could make her stop bleeding.

"What do I do, Mom?" Helplessness consumed me. "We only have jerky and water. I don't know where the last of our food went. It's literally all gone. Everything." I held up the canteen and the small plastic bag of chipotle flavored beef jerky.

"Let's drink some water and eat something. Then we can try to sleep. I'm so tired, aren't you?" Her eyelids drooped and shadows dwarfed her eyes. I had never seen her so weak. The sight scared the living crap out of me.

I nodded. "Yeah, but I need to go to the bathroom, first. Do you need to go?"

She allowed her eyes to close again. "No. Not right now." Her lips parted and she fell asleep. When she woke up, I would get her to eat or at least suck on a piece of jerky and sip some water. Sleep for her would be good so her body could repair itself. Her need to sleep had to be a good thing.

Barely afternoon and as exhausted as I was, no way would I be able to sleep. Not as amped up as the day had made me.

Plus, I really did need to pee.

Careful not to wake Mom, I stood and exited the shop wing, closing the door behind me to preserve heat.

My cottony mouth irritated me with its flavor. What I wouldn't give for a toothbrush and toothpaste – oh, and a shower.

I fell to the river rock on the grass outside the back door. Tears filled my eyes and my breathing hitched. I rocked back and forth on my knees, bending at the waist, wrapping my arms tight to my chest.

The sobs came, long and low, from deep in my gut. Too much. I was losing too much. Why hadn't the pain killed me yet? I should be dead from so much loss. So much anguish.

What was I going to do?

And then I tried it. I prayed. And prayed. And prayed.

If nothing else, the prayers at least made me feel better. I recited one from a book my mom had given me when I was younger. Something about laying myself down to sleep, blah blah blah.

I didn't even remember all the words so I mixed them together with Rock-a-bye Baby.

After I calmed down enough to realize I still hadn't peed, I ducked behind some lilac bushes and did my job. I avoided looking at the house. Nothing would make me go in there, not even my hunger. Not yet. At least while Mom slept. When she got better we could go in together. What if Bodey's family was dead in there? No. Just. No.

I couldn't return to sit vigil over my mom just yet. Exploring seemed the best bet for my nerves. Maybe I could find something to eat. Or something to do.

Something to keep my mind off our situation.

Anything to keep me sane.

B. R. PAULSON

CHAPTER 16

Someone shook my shoulder. My head flopped to the side and my chin connected with my chest. I jerked myself upright, eyes open but quickly shutting again. I hadn't slept long enough.

"Kelly, wake up, please, wake up." Mom's thready whisper broke through the haze of my sleepiness.

My eyes opened and this time they didn't slip down. Alarmed, I reached for her outstretched hand. "Mom? Are you okay?" I shifted myself to a fuller sitting position. She had somehow fallen from the slightly raised platform where I had made her a bed. I pushed myself to her side and pulled her seemingly frail body onto my lap.

Pale skin, palest I'd ever seen on her, enunciated the shadows of her eyes. I never noticed the strands of gray in her hair so distinctly before. "Mom?" I wiped a stray chunk of hair from her forehead, a cool clamminess meeting my touch. "You're colder. Hold on, I'll get you covered up…" But her hand on mine stilled me.

"No. I don't need…" She swallowed, visibly aching even to talk. A fresh, bright red spread across her shirt, slowly but with intent. "Let's pray, Kelly. Would you?" Her voice faded and she lifted her hands to her chest, like in a prayer position, but loose.

Anger welled inside me and I pushed her hands from her chest, mindful of her pain but oddly apathetic toward it. "No, I'm not praying with you anymore. This is ridiculous. We've prayed for food, water, medicine, for your wound to get better, you name it, we've *prayed* for it. I'm done. It's gotten us nothing. Less than nothing. We've been chewing on jerky. I can't." I couldn't even continue with my rant, my heart rate sped up and the fact I was yelling at my injured mother finally kicked in and I bit my tongue. Dang it. I wasn't trying to be disrespectful, but come on.

We sat together in silence for a second, Mom staring at me with eyes wide in disbelief.

My throat tightened. She might be gone soon. Her wounds could prevent her from bugging me anymore. The injustice of our situation slammed home. Why would she have so much faith in anyone or anything with all the destruction and pain around us – in us? I blinked back frustrated tears. "Do you really think there's a God?" My husky question didn't hesitate to be insecure, but the honesty left me drained as the truth of my doubt revealed itself.

Suddenly her eyes narrowed and she struggled to lift herself. Even though she didn't move much, she appeared to have grown larger, stronger, defiant in seconds. She coughed, gripping at her side. "I don't think – I *know* – there's a God. There's a Heaven where your dad and brother are waiting for us."

"Let them wait. We're not ready. We aren't going anywhere." I growled. What was she saying? Heaven? Who mentioned Heaven? What was going on?

"Stop." She pierced me with her gaze, sharp and deceptively strong in a body worn down with a gunshot injury. "I only have my faith and I can't give that to you. And you're going to be mad at me and God and that's okay. Just know…" She captured my hand in hers and pressed my fingers tight to her chest, tears welling in her eyes.

I couldn't cry, I couldn't. Yet, my love for her dripped down my face.

"Know that we *both* love you and we're always here." She closed her eyes and shook, a shiver spasming through her body. She reopened her eyes and focused on me. She forcefully swallowed. "Remember the rules, Kelly. Trust no one. Pray. And please, *please*, stay alive." She pressed her hand to just over my heart, tears streaming back over her temples and into her hair.

I sniffed, shaking my head to cut her off. "Mom."

"Kelly, *stay alive*. Please. I'm always here." She tapped one finger on my chest, but her hand dropped to her side and her face fell slack. Slowly her head turned toward my arm and her chest lowered with her last exhale.

Disbelief jerked me from the surreal pain and thrust me into the moment hard. "Mom? Mommy, no. Mom! No!" I shook her softly at first, then with more force. Tears? There was no term strong enough for the torrent soaking my skin and dripping onto her face. "Mom, please. Don't leave me."

She *wasn't* always here. She wasn't *with* me anymore. She'd just gone and left. Gone. Like everyone else.

Mom, where are you? I need you. Please. I watched her, but she didn't move. Nothing moved on her. We were attached but she'd left me. I didn't even get to tell her how much I loved her, needed her.

"I love you, Mom. I'm sorry. Please, come back." I sobbed, wrapping my arms around her and pulling her to my chest. *Please. Oh, Lord, please.*

I was alone. And there was nothing I could do about it.

The pain built and built until I couldn't take the pressure anymore – I screamed.

B. R. PAULSON

CHAPTER 17

I don't know how long I held Mom's body. How long I brushed her hair from her face and pretended she slept. I crooned to her, talked to her, even yelled at her a couple times. But she didn't wake up. She didn't move.

My legs had fallen asleep but I didn't care. My mom…

Dead.

How many more people would die in my arms? I wiped at my face with the sleeve of my sweatshirt. I couldn't bring myself to leave her. Did I even care anymore what happened to me?

The sound of a car door slamming rebounded off the front of the shop. I tensed, every muscle in my body tightening.

Why couldn't I catch a break? Was this some kind of game where people followed me and threw curve balls my way to make sure I never got rest? I had lost everyone. If this was some kind of dream where I'd fallen into a black hole and everything disappeared around me, I would sincerely like to wake up now.

But waking up would be too easy. Bad, worse, worst. The order of how things went.

A sick feeling in my stomach warned me I hadn't reached *worst* yet.

I had nowhere to hide Mom, not even enough time to, if I could. I didn't want to leave her though either. She was still warm and if I ignored the fact that she wasn't moving, I could believe she was asleep.

Maybe the noise had been a trick of my imagination and I hadn't heard anything.

Muffled yelling came from the direction of the back door of the shop. A man's voice thundered through the walls. "I can't believe this!"

A bang and I jumped. Lifting Mom the best I could from my lap, I searched all around for a place to hide. Standing on legs which didn't want to do anything because they'd long past lost feeling, I kicked and stamped my feet as soft as possible and stepped toward the carpet rolls, ducking behind them seconds before the door opened to the room.

Carpet scratched my cheeks. I leaned against the soft insulation and jerked back. Dad had once said insulation was made from spun glass. I wanted to close my eyes, but I couldn't. I was the stupid person who watched the axe swing down to decapitate me. Surprises weren't my thing.

"Crap! Dad, there's an injured woman in here!" He rushed to Mom's side.

Dead, she's dead. Not injured. Not anymore.

Icy truth froze my sadness. Between the rolls of carpet, I could barely make out his hands checking her neck for a pulse. He hung his head, blond hair coming into view.

A new voice arrived at the door. "She's hurt?"

The boy moved his head out of my line of sight. I stared at Mom, unable to look away.

His hands left the small window of my view. "No. I mean, yes she's hurt, but she's not… she's dead."

Fingers snapped.

The boy disappeared. My mom used to snap her fingers to get Braden's and my attention. I didn't even look up. If I stared long enough, her chest would suddenly start moving and she would stand up, laughing like everything was a dang joke.

The carpet rolls started falling away. I hadn't touched them enough to move them. I darted to the side, but a man blocked the way with a roll leaning in his arms. I didn't look up. I couldn't. I needed to escape.

I squeaked and turned the other way, running smack into the solid chest of the boy. Shaking, I couldn't stop. I crossed my arms and backed up, staring at the ground. I didn't want to be caught. I wasn't ready for anything else bad to happen.

Just give me a minute. I couldn't breathe. Mom, I needed my mom. *Mom, help.*

And I wanted – no, needed time to mourn my mom.

I couldn't wait any longer. I lost my control. Sobbing racked my body and I slid to the ground, arms tight, fingers gripping my elbows. I was full into ugly cry mode, baring my teeth and everything. I didn't give a crap.

"Kelly? Oh, my word, Dad. It's Kelly Williams from school." The boy knelt beside me, pulling me into his arms. I flinched, but couldn't pull away, too much energy went into my crying, my loss. Survival mode had redirected and I blocked stuff out.

"Kelly, shh, Kelly, you're okay. Look at me. Come on, look at me." He shifted me away from him for a moment so I could look into his face.

Bodey Christianson came into focus when I opened my eyes.

I couldn't control the relief mixing with increased shock and I slumped forward onto his shoulder, wrapping my arms around his waist. Someone I know! Someone familiar. And he wasn't dead.

Something wasn't *worse*. Finally.

I don't remember what time I fell asleep on him, but it must have been soon after falling into his arms.

~~~

Softness and the scent of vanilla surrounded me like a cloud. I didn't want to open my eyes because all the comfort would go away. It had to. Everything else in my world had gone away.

I stretched and pushed against smooth, cool sheets. *Don't wake up, Kelly, don't.* When was the last time I slept so well? Slept hard enough I could talk myself back from opening my eyes.

Yawning, I rolled over, reveling in the comfort of the bed.

Bed? Yes, I was definitely in a bed. Did Mom know —

I jerked upright, eyes snapping open. My gaze focused on the cream colored wall across the room from me. The bedroom wasn't overly female or male. Neutral colors of cream and tan with an accent of blue in the curtains confused me. Even the comforter and sheet set didn't lean in a gender-specific direction.

Where was I and how had I gotten there? I remembered Bodey and crying like a freak all over him.

And Mom. How could her death have momentarily slipped my mind? Not when she died in my arms, reminding me to pray, not trust anyone, and survive.

Shame flooded me. I wasn't going to stay alive, if I couldn't pinpoint where I was or the circumstances which had brought me to the room. I had trusted Bodey enough to pass out in his arms. If Mom was still alive, what would I say? I know the boy? Kind of. Had always wanted to know him more, so I hoped he would ask me to stay with them. Something.

Because I'd never been more alone.

Why did they leave me by myself? Did they trust me? Why would they? Bodey didn't know me well and his dad didn't know me at all. I'm sure he didn't remember me from my one-time visit to drop off information for his son. Why would he?

I rubbed my fingers over the stitching of the quilt, ignoring the ache in my shoulders as I slouched over my straight legs. How long had I slept? Thick curtains blacked out the majority of the light, letting only enough through a slit between the two panels to see clearly without being over-bright.

Careful not to ruin the bedding or anything with my rough jeans, I slid from the sheets. I searched the floor for my jacket and shoes, grateful that whoever had brought me hadn't undressed me. Folded carefully and placed on the chair, my jacket seemed unassuming and almost normal. Like nothing had happened. Like my mom had picked the item from the floor and softly reproached me to take care of my things.

For one second, I let myself believe she'd been in my room, shaking her head as she'd folded the sleeves of my coat together.

Lifting my hands to rebraid my hair, I flinched at the sight of bloodstains on my fingers and palms – wow, even up my wrists to my elbows. Mom's blood. Jeanine hadn't allowed me to touch her, brushing me off with comments like she was fine and didn't need help. Mom had, though. She worried about me going too far from her because she wanted to keep her eye on me, even when she could barely move.

All-consuming silence soothed my fears. How could anything be wrong, when no one screamed or cried or things weren't blowing up? Unless, I was all alone again. Suddenly, I had to know. Was I alone? Had they left me?

I remade the bed and claimed my jacket, pulling the sleeves on to keep my hands free. I had to prepare for the reality. Bodey and his dad might be gone. Mom was. Jeanine was. Dad and Braden were. Denying the things which could happen, had happened, was only setting myself up for more disappointment, harsher loss.

Opening the door slowly, I looked out the door to the right and the left. Would I find an office harboring a fatally shot man at a desk? Would I discover Bodey and his father dead somewhere while their killers looted the place?

A soft woof pulled my attention down the hall. One of the Labs I had greeted at my first visit approached me, tail wagging almost as fast as his tongue moved in and out of his mouth. I bent my knees and crouched to his level, scratching his neck and behind his ears. I swallowed back more tears. Between Bodey and his dad and the dog, I could almost say I knew what it was like to see someone back from the dead.

The dog's entire body wagged back and forth as he turned to skip alongside me. I tiptoed down the hall toward what I hoped was the front of the house. Where had everyone gone?

Soft clinking of glass on glass reassured me someone was still in the house. I wasn't alone. Not completely. Even if they didn't want me to stay or be around them for long, at least I had *someone* for a few minutes.

Pushing through a swinging door, I entered the kitchen decorated with warm wood tones. A double oven manned the wall beside the door. Bodey stood at the counter with a sandwich in one hand and a dog treat in the other. He stopped mid-smile when his gaze met mine. He nodded carefully my way like I wouldn't understand the moment or the need to feel happiness when something so terrible had recently happened.

His dad rinsed out a cup at the sink. He turned at the sudden silence in the room. Similar in coloring to Bodey, his features softened at my arrival. He lifted his eyebrow, setting the mug down on the counter. "Hello, Kelly. Bodey has told me a lot about you."

I glanced sharply at Bodey. Even with everything going on the fact he had known enough about me to say things to his dad warmed me. Like I hadn't been the only one noticing the other.

Bodey's cheeks flushed. He bit into the sandwich, shrugging.

"I'm sorry for your loss. Her wound looked like she was shot." Mr. Christianson crossed his arms over his chest and leaned his hip against the counter. Until that moment, I hadn't realized how nervous I was. With his relaxed pose, I allowed myself to shed some discomfort.

"Thank you." I think. How did one answer condolences? I hadn't seen Mom since I crashed on Bodey. I'd broken into their shop and as it turned out, for nothing. I couldn't save my mom, no matter where I took her. I ruined their window in vain.

I cleared my throat, suddenly embarrassed, but aware something needed to be said. "I'm sorry for breaking your window to get into your shop. It was… I thought… Maybe getting out…" I shrugged. "We were chased. Mom had set us up with a co-op before…" I waved my hand in the air like everything was happening and right there for me to encompass all of it with my hand movements. "This stuff. When we got up there after the bombs in Post Falls and the actual leader isn't even alive and Mom had to…" Even though what she'd done was nothing to be ashamed of, I couldn't share *that*, not *that*. Some things belonged to people and didn't need to be spread among others. Mom's privacy, especially in death, suddenly seemed more important than simple details which wouldn't help anyone in the long run.

His dad kicked at the ground, but watched me. "So you were with a group. Did something happen to them?"

"No, Mr. Christianson. The group turned out to be, well, not what Mom had planned on. Things were getting out of hand and one of the other women who was, let's say, used incorrectly, said the main guy planned on trading me and some of the other women for supplies." I avoided Bodey's eyes. Shame flooded me. I hadn't even done anything. Embarrassment flushed my skin because someone else had treated me like property and I hadn't consented.

Bodey couldn't think less of me. Why did I still care so much what he thought? Because I liked him. Tons.

Mr. Christianson shoved away from the counter. Holding out his hand, he smiled warmly at me. "No, call me John. I have a feeling we're going to be seeing a lot more of each other. The Mr. Christianson thing is going to get old fast."

I stared at him, doubt squinting my eyes. "You don't want me to leave?"

He glanced at his son, a soft chuckle breaking my tense question's pause. "Where would you go? What kind of a man would I be sending a child out into this?" He pointed his finger at the window. "No one is making it. We've been back into town to help and there's nothing. No one." A shadow passed over his eyes and he stared at his feet.

Bodey looked away from both of us, his features tight. I would recognize loss anywhere, I lived loss like a fashion trend. The sting didn't lessen. Instead the pain increased like a burning brand while the nerves continued to heat, damaging more and more.

"I'm sorry." I didn't need to expand. Their loss was none of my business. If they hadn't seen me with my mom's body, I probably wouldn't have told them – or anyone – about my loss.

We stood together in discordant silence as we took in the somberness of the moment.

John broke into our thoughts. "I know this isn't something you want to think about, but we need to do something with… your mom. Can we bury her? Or do you want to do something else?"

What else would we do? Like we had the option for cremation, unless of course, John meant some kind of a Viking funeral pyre.

Bodey polished off his sandwich. "What else would we do, Dad? We don't have a lot of options out here." His tone was respectful and curious. I'd never heard anyone speak like that to their parent. In school, everyone had a tone which dripped with condescension toward their mothers or fathers.

I had brought the disrespectful attitude home more than once and Mom hadn't freaked out or even reacted much. But I regretted them, all of them, including so many other moments I took her for granted. Why hadn't anyone warned me? How had I not learned about life's fragility when my dad died? I only grew more surly and rude.

I scratched at the back of my hand like my shame had localized below my wrist.

"Well, I guess what I'm asking without being too blunt, is do you want to be there when I bury the body or would you rather talk about her here and let me do what needs to be done? Either one is fine. Your mom was a slight woman, so moving her will be easy. I don't want to step on your feet with what you'd prefer." John moved his hands when he spoke, something I remember Bodey doing when he grew impassioned about a topic in track.

"I want to help, please." I couldn't allow someone else to take care of her. No, I had to be there. I had to see her body one last time, accept that she wasn't in it anymore.

"Okay, let me go get things ready. Bodey, can you find Kelly something to eat? Dress warm, the sun's going down. We'll do the service about sunset." He smiled and softly touched my shoulder when he passed. Something about the lines around his mouth reminded me of my dad. "Oh, and bring anything you might want to leave with her – some kind of a token or something."

Oh, the intense longings for Dad hit at the worst times. Right then, was definitely the worst.

I shifted my feet, holding one elbow in my hand. When I wanted to talk to Bodey, I didn't want him to talk to me because his dad told him to. Dang, I couldn't return his smile because everything seemed forced from his side.

"How about a sandwich? I can make a mean roast beef and since we don't have very much fuel for the generator left, we need to use the meat." He grinned, a dimple in his cheek disarming me enough to bring out my own hesitant smile.

He moved around the kitchen, putting together a sandwich with items from the fridge and a bread box on the counter beside the window. Bodey set a plate at a spot on the island counter and motioned me forward. Chips and a pickle slice rounded out the meal and I sat, staring at the abundance.

"Is everything okay? I mean besides... I mean is the sandwich okay? Do you eat roast beef?" He wrung his hands, the twisting enhancing the muscles in his forearms. He glanced from me to the sandwich and back.

I nodded, resting my lower arms against the table. I didn't want to eat the sandwich because I was so hungry and so nervous I would never see another one like it. "I love roast beef, thank you."

But I couldn't eat. Emotion welled in my chest and I tried breathing deep to keep any more embarrassing displays down.

His voice low, Bodey leaned on the counter across from me and ducked his head to capture my gaze. "I really am sorry about your mom, Kelly."

Tears moistened my eyes and I nodded. "Thanks."

He twiddled with a fork left on the counter. "We can't find my mom or my sister. We keep going back but..." Speaking matter-of-factly, Bodey shrugged. "We keep hoping, you know? But the not-knowing is tough."

I could only imagine. At least I knew where my family was. Dead had to be better than traded around in Charlie's personal slavery trade. Impulsively, I reached across the counter and grasped Bodey's hand in mine. "I'm sorry." I swallowed. "I thought you were dead. That… hurt." Sharing too much didn't seem possible with the world burning around us, in the face of our personal losses.

As vulnerable as it made me, I needed to take time to tell someone, anyone, how important they were. Since it was Bodey, who I crushed on for years, the moment was even more poignant.

His blond hair fell into his eyes and he shook his head to move the strands out of the way. He returned the pressure of my fingers. "I've never been so happy to see someone. I'm sorry. That sounds bad, but I'm glad it was you."

He rounded the counter and wrapped his arm around my waist, pressing his cheek to the top of my head.

Like a brother.

Crap.

CHAPTER 18

My fingers tightened around the leather binding of Mom's Bible. Between the book and guns I packed into the fanny pack which detached from my backpack, I could've been channeling her spirit. Hoped I was.

The cool afternoon air hinted of an upcoming storm, an occasional chill on the breeze. We were far enough north that the canopy overhead splintered the light with needles and cones.

John smiled encouragingly at me as I approached the edge of the clearing on the far side of the drive. His plan to place Mom by the Aspen copse outside of view of the house seemed illogical until the picturesque scenery of white trunks and green coin-sized leaves fluttering in the slight wind came into view.

Long green stalks of grass reached for the lowest branches of the trees, seed fluff bending and waving in the air.

Dark brown dirt spotted with gray river rock had been piled neatly beside a long, three-foot deep hole. John had lined the hole with a camouflage canvas material, almost like a tarp.

Grimacing at the place we would lay my mom to rest, I glanced toward the house. Bodey walked toward us, carrying Mom's slight body in his arms. When had she become so small a young man could easily bear her weight?

The sudden realization hit me that I'd missed out on a lot in the last two years, as I wrapped myself in condescension, patronizing humor, and downright disrespect for Mom and anything else resembling authority.

Her rules had irritated me. Their constant repetition growing on my nerves with their redundancy. The more I thought about them, the smarter they were. She hadn't followed them – at least the trusting-no-one rule.

Oh, as well as the one which clearly stated *stay alive*. Couldn't forget how she ditched that particular rule.

What I wouldn't give to hear her repeat those rules again. And again. And again.

I fingered the corner of her well-read Bible. Her favorite scripture had been highlighted and tagged and even notated with her own comments in the margins. Hopeful I could read the verse over her body before we lowered it. I moved to stand beside John.

Bodey rounded the two of us, pushing through the collection of weeds and grasses. He set her on the ground, wrapping her completely with a faded quilt, covering her face with the corner.

"Wait." I rushed forward, shifting the blanket from her skin to see that she was gone. I had to make sure. She looked so peaceful, even her bruises and scrapes seemed faded as the skin around her eyes wasn't tight and her mouth wasn't surrounded by lines.

"Do you want to say a prayer or anything?" John's murmur set the tone of reverence and I nodded, replacing the blanket and returning to his side. Gratitude filled me, someone else took the reins of the distasteful affair. I never attended a funeral or a memorial service before.

Dad and Braden had died when everyone else was dying. We spoke of them in our living room, with curtains blocking out the light for two days. Most of the houses in the nation and the world had done the same as they lost one or more of their family members.

We weren't special.

In the forest, we weren't any different. Except, we were going to *bury* Mom. So many other people would never see their loved ones put to rest.

I didn't have any tears left, at least not right at that second. Mom's passing in my arms had sucked me dry and with her face covered she almost disappeared – became less her and more *absent*.

We bowed our heads and folded our hands. Was I supposed to say it? Or was he going to?

I parted my lips, not sure what to say but certain the words would come to me. They had to, right?

A shot echoed off the house and trees. John pushed at Bodey's shoulder and wrapped his arm around my waist, pulling me down beside him on the ground. We hid behind the brush lining the clearing, catching glimpses of the backs of men as they surrounded the house.

One of the dogs yelped as a man kicked him. His gun came up fast and he rang off another shot, dropping the animal I had been so excited to see.

The man laughed, kicking the downed body across the dirt. That laugh. That voice. I scooted backward until the soft, newly dug dirt cushioned my grasping fingers.

Meeting John's questioning gaze with my own, I shook my head with short jerks and swallowed.

Charlie had found me. How? I'd been so careful. I waited in that stupid roundabout until no one had been around. What was he doing at the Christianson home?

The other men with him pushed doors open and stomped through the house. Bodey crab-walked to my side and gripped my hand. He murmured softer than the grass rustling in the breeze. "It's okay. We'll be okay."

Another shot from inside the home.

"They got Abigail." Their other dog. Bodey's words were louder, but not by much. He moved to get his legs under him and stand.

John pressed his hand to Bodey's chest. His whisper held more firmness than if he yelled. "Stay. Nothing is worth getting shot." He motioned for us to sit calmly. "We'll wait until they leave. We're okay here."

We sat, waiting for the men to leave. Each gunshot brought a flinch and finally closed my eyes to wait them out.

A whoop from the back of the shop made me look. A different guy charged from the garage toward Charlie, holding a pack – Mom's pack – above his head.

Charlie roared, yanking the bag from his man's hands. "She's here. They're here. Find them. I want them found, now!" The men scattered like chicken, as if somehow the secret to Mom's whereabouts lay in the front yard of the house or the deck. They searched like small children, walking back and forth.

Brandishing a pistol, Charlie stormed through the group of eight men. "If you don't start looking, I'm going to shoot one of you. Then another. I want *them* found."

I bit my lip. Charlie wouldn't give up. He would search until he destroyed everything or found us.

Smoke furled around the northern-most corner of the house. I glanced at John. His jaw clenched, his forearms tight and rippling.

"Dad, they're burning our home. Our things." Bodey's tortured gasp matched the sickening twist in my gut. His whisper hurt my chest.

Because of me. I bit my lip, then murmured, "I can go. He might stop, if he has me."

John placed his hand on my arm. "No. If those men want you, they'll have to find you and get through us." He pushed Bodey's chest. "Go.

Get past the back corner. We're prepared for this." He glanced back over the grasses. "Follow him, Kelly. Let's go."

He angled his head to block my straying gaze. "Don't look back. Just go." Sadness flattened under his resolve, his strength enabling me to move and do as he said.

Bodey crawled past the grave and Mom. He didn't stand until well into the forest and out of sight of the house. John passed me as I slowed beside my mom's body. I didn't want to leave her. I didn't want to say goodbye on Charlie's terms. She was my mom and I hadn't been able to save her. She died because of me.

John paused beside me. He patted Mom's shoulder and then mine. Keeping his voice low, his words washed over me. "I'm not your mom or your dad, Kelly, but I promise to watch over you like my own." He bent his head and murmured to my mom. "I'll watch over your daughter. We need to leave though, so it's goodbye for now." He touched her head and met my gaze.

Tears I thought dried up wet my eyes. I nodded at him, sniffing. Tucking her Bible into the fanny pack, I leaned down and kissed the quilt over her face. I didn't want to see her blank expression or limp features.

Following John, I didn't look back. There was nothing for me there.

Not anymore.

CHAPTER 19

We stopped hiking beside a covered, well-stacked pile of fire wood. John pulled down the back wall of logs and revealed a cavity filled with supplies.

"Only take what you can comfortably carry. We should have enough backpacks in here for each of us. I don't have any extra blankets. So the two in each pack will need to do." He handed me a black and green hiking pack, similar to the one I used of my dad's. I pulled the straps on. He nodded my way. "You have my wife's. She's about the same size you are. So you can use the extra clothes in there."

He turned away before I could reply. What would I say? Thanks for giving me your wife's stuff? She's probably dead like my mom, but thanks just the same? He would understand the sentiment but I couldn't say anything, the words awkward and heavy on my tongue.

Bodey pulled on a pack of his own, grabbing a canteen and draping the long shoulder strap around his neck and over one arm. His dad did the same.

Copying them, I grabbed a canteen and pulled it over my head, the nylon lines scratching my skin.

John handed me a camouflage bucket hat with a cord to tighten under my chin. "To keep the sun off you, if it ever comes back out." He pulled out of the cavity and stacked the few logs to reseal the storage space. "Let's go, kids."

Bodey fell into step behind me, the slight huff of his breath a comfort as I followed John from their property. We headed into the forest, more shots from the direction of the house chasing us down a rise and into a ravine.

Hopefully, John knew where we were going, because I'd exhausted any plans I could've come up with. I didn't know what to do or where to go, but I could place one foot in front of the other and follow the Christiansons out of there.

John had promised to take care of me. The short time with Mom in camp had taught me I needed support in some form. We all seemed to.

~~~

Thankfully my boots fit well. We walked and walked, climbing over rock and shale mountain slides where walking wasn't probable. Ducking under fallen trees and leaving the faint game trail when overgrowth refused to allow us to pass, we pressed forward, following John's lead.

We didn't speak much. I'm not sure when silence with those men became comfortable. It wasn't the norm for me, to be comfortable with just anyone. Maybe the circumstances forced us, or the promise from John had torn down all walls that would have kept me at bay.

Stopping under a boulder overhang, we all took a seat on the moss-covered rocky ground and closed our eyes. Soon the sun would set, minutes really, and the shadows didn't give any hint as to the direction we traveled.

I slid the bag off my back, careful to check the pack clipped around my waist for Mom's guns and Bible. I pulled out the book, longing to touch something of hers she'd held so dear.

Opening the cover, I stared at the family picture we had taken weeks before Dad and Braden had gone south. Mom had taped the photo inside the Bible and covered it with clear packaging tape to protect the surface. In blue ink she had written the date and our names, looping the Ls. Tracing her script with my forefinger, I couldn't ignore the choking sensation in my throat and chest or the sadness filling my eyes.

No one else cried. No one else lost their control. John and Bodey had no idea where the rest of their family was. That would be worse. Bad was what I had. Worse is what they had.

I didn't want to know what worst could be.

Swigging from the canteen, I licked my lips. The water had been in the aluminum container a while with its stale aftertaste and metallic bite. But I didn't stop. I needed more. A fine sweat covered me and an ache in my muscles griped at me for walking so far, over-working muscles not completely rested from fleeing with Mom.

Bodey panted, wiping his forehead. "I haven't run in a while. Good pace, Dad."

John laughed. He clapped Bodey on the upper shoulder. "Struggling to keep up with your old man, huh? That makes me feel good, even if you are exaggerating."

I lowered my water and watched their easy rapport. I never had ease with my mom, even when the rest of our family had been around. We always acted like a ruler separated us and we could never get closer than twelve inches or so.

The three of us fell into silence, the dark slipping over us.

"Are we going to have a fire?" I couldn't help asking. Not knowing what we were doing and leaving it in someone else's hands was harder than I'd thought.

John shook his head. "No. It brings too much attention. We're not stopping here longer than necessary. We need to get to a more stable shelter."

Guilt overcame me. I had to apologize again. "I'm sorry. They were there for me. Nothing would've happened to your place, if I stayed away." We wouldn't be looking for shelter, or they wouldn't.

"Stayed away? Do you think they knew you were there? I guarantee they had no idea." John shook his head, cradling the canteen in his hands. "No, they were looking for trouble. Bodey and I saw that guy at another place. We were able to get out. It was only a matter of time before they'd head up toward our place."

Yeah, I understood what he was saying. Charlie and his gang looted. They didn't have an original idea in their heads. They stole the camp and the investors as well as the things to run it with.

Where would we go, though?

"Take a few more minutes, you two. Then we need to get going again." He leaned his head back against the rocky wall and held his water in his empty hand. A dad was there – he wasn't my dad, but he was a dad and he had our safety in mind. I hadn't been comforted like that in a long time.

Bodey dug into his pack and pulled out a granola bar. Holding the snack toward me, he smiled. "Dad'll sleep for a little bit, if you want to try and get some rest. I never do because naps always make me more tired." He smiled and it was like the last few days hadn't happened as a flush of warmth covered me. He used to smile at me in track, too, and my insides had gone all mushy then as well.

I took the treat and looked at my hands. "I don't nap very well, either. Thank you."

A stocking hat pushed the shaggy ends of his dirty blond hair down around his face, framing his strong jaw and brilliant blue eyes.

He'd passed the awkward adolescent phase his junior year – my sophomore year. I remember the first time I saw him after summer break when he came in for a cross country meeting. My friend had pushed my arm because my mouth had fallen open and I stared.

Broad shoulders atop a wide chest tapered down into a tight waist. My cheeks had flamed too warm for me to look further. Okay, I peeked, but that's all I'm going to comment on. He'd turned from talking to the boys' coach and met my gaze. Dark lashes had mesmerized me and when he grinned and waved, I'd lifted my fingers but hadn't smiled or anything. I froze.

He inclined his head and then turned and joined the boys.

I pretty much avoided him the rest of the season out of sheer embarrassment.

Bodey bit into his bar, watching out the overhang entrance. Forearms resting on his knees, he lost all expression in his face and the skin around his eyes tightened. "I'm sorry about your mom, Kelly."

I didn't want to talk about my mom. Not yet. "Thanks." He already said that anyway. I bit into my own granola bar and stared in the same direction as him. For once, I wanted him not to talk to me. Sitting in silence with him would be perfect. I wouldn't be alone, but I also could lose myself in my thoughts.

He seemed to read my mind and together we watched the darkness fall completely and the stars peek above the tree line.

Kind of a crazy first date. I would never tell him I was going to count it as a date. He'd probably think I was insane. He'd be right.

~~~

John pushed a branch out of my way, letting the bough swing back to place after I passed. "Bodey, you and Kelly need to stay close. I'm not sure if town is safe yet."

The moon hid behind clouds, making travel slower than by day. John refused to allow flashlights so we made our way as carefully as possible. I understood the no-lights rule. I also understood pain from tripping and falling.

He half-explained traveling at night would be the best in our situation. I got what he was saying, but I didn't like it. Bodey didn't either.

One thing I liked about Bodey though was his deep respect for his dad. He wouldn't say he didn't like something because he understood John wouldn't make us walk all night for fun. Bodey walked forward, following his dad and me with no complaints.

Even when I tripped over a collection of rocks trying to assassinate me. Did I fall forward like a normal girl would? No, of course not, I had to over-correct myself, hyperextend my knee, and fall backwards, landing on Bodey and causing us both to fall to the trail.

He grunted when my elbow landed smack in the middle of his stomach, under his diaphragm.

I rolled off him as fast as I could, heat in my face. "I'm so sorry. Are you okay? I didn't mean…" Of course I hadn't meant to. He knew, right?

Bodey reached out, cradling my elbows in his warm hands. He steadied me, waiting until I calmed down and held still. A soft side smile reached the corners of his eyes. "You're okay. Don't worry about me. You're not big enough to hurt me. Are you hurt?"

Hurt? What could be hurting while he touched me? "Me? I'm not sure." Yep, I was a brilliant conversationalist. At that rate, he'd fall in love with me in about eighty years.

Oh, where was my mom to laugh about all the awkwardness with? I blinked. Crap, was I staring again?

My knee ached, but not so bad I couldn't stand on the leg. "I think I'm fine." I searched his face in the dark. "Thank you. Again, sorry." How many times would I apologize for being a klutz? Who knew how many more forest things would attack me in the dark?

"Are you two okay? Let's keep going." John had picked up a long straight branch sometime back which he used as a walking stick.

I pushed away from Bodey against my better judgment and followed John. The twinge in my knee grew more prominent. I limped as we went up a slight rise, then down. Small tree trunks offered stable grips as I passed, using each as pieces to a modified railing. I didn't want to fall again.

We hadn't heard anyone behind us since we left the wood stack. As pain sharpened in my knee, I debated asking John if we could stop, but slowing us down or stopping wouldn't help the group. I ground my teeth as each step increased my pain.

My limp turned to a hobble and I desperately wanted to switch Bodey places so he wouldn't watch me turn handicapped before his eyes. Plus, part of me wanted to lie down and cry. I might not be able to lie down, but as long as he could see me, I certainly wouldn't be able to cry either.

Bodey wrapped his arm around my waist, taking weight off my leg. "Dad, we need to stop." The adorable boy had to be a mind reader. He helped me get to a bigger tree.

John paused, turning to look back at us. I leaned against the trunk, wanting to scream thank you to the heavens but careful to keep my mouth closed.

I wouldn't complain. I wouldn't complain. I wouldn't complain.

Oh man, the break was very much needed.

Bodey passed me and stood close to John. They peeked back at me as they whispered to each other.

Could they be any more obvious? I closed my eyes so I wouldn't see them discuss me. The pain in my knee overrode my desire to be easygoing.

They approached my place of refuge, rock crunching on rock warning me to open my eyes. I braced myself for sympathy. Since I didn't know them well, I didn't know what to expect, but they had been kind so far. They wouldn't hurt me, but would they try to carry me? Just thinking about that sent a wave of embarrassed tingling from my toes to the back of my head.

"Kelly, Bodey says you're limping. Can I look at your knee?" John bent down, waiting for me to push my injured leg toward him. He didn't lift my pants, what would he see in the dark anyway, but he gently pressed around my kneecap and behind the bend.

I flinched when his thumb pressed into the soft tissue to the inside of my leg.

John stood. "Okay, I think you twisted your knee, which shouldn't be permanent but could get worse, if we don't let it rest. Let's find a place to camp and we'll do what we can."

"Where? There's not much here." Bodey opened his arms wide and turned in a circle.

"Athol's right through there." John pointed past the next bend in the trees. "We'll check and see if there's a place we can hide out for a while. Bodey, grab her other side, will ya?"

They flanked me, each pulling my arm around their necks and half-carrying me as we walked. At least they didn't completely immobilize me. I had to be able to carry some of my weight. If not, survival of the fittest didn't apply to me at all.

The path wasn't wide enough for all of us and Bodey or John would lurch forward in the weeds, tripping over hidden rocks and roots.

The last stagger brought us all down. I'm not sure who went first, but John landed on my leg and I cried out, reaching for the offended part.

"Alright, this isn't working." John scrambled off me, holding out his hand to Bodey. "Give me your pack, Kelly. Bodey, if you'll grab her, I can lead. We'll take turns until we find something."

Bodey hefted me into his arms. I never realized how strong he was. I mean, muscles, yeah, but I never considered them as functional – just beautiful. When he had carried Mom, the thought never crossed my mind because she looked so slight.

He found a rhythm with his pace. I tried holding myself stiff with my head up and my back tight, but the rolling lumber of his steps sucked at me. I had been awake for too long and gone through too much. This time I wouldn't fall asleep.

Finally in Bodey's arms, no way was I going to miss a second of it.

~~~

Athol appeared after no more than five minutes of solid walking. Finding a safe place to hole up proved to be more difficult. John refused to let us stay in any stores where food was commonly stocked. The pawn shop and second-hand store didn't make the cut either since those places traditionally carried supplies.

Bodey and John hadn't switched me between them. I was extremely comfortable staying in Bodey's arms. I just hoped he didn't mind.

John finally settled on the flooring store and when he jimmied the backdoor, I lifted my eyebrows at Bodey. Why would we stay in a carpet store? How odd.

Bodey wiggled his eyebrows back at me and twisted his lips, baring his teeth. I giggled. Held so close in his arms, with my hands hooked around his neck, I refused to believe the proximity was sibling-like.

Would he notice I hadn't showered in a few days and I probably didn't smell right? Oh, I could see myself praying about that. The thought kept me from completely relaxing.

"Come in, guys, the building's empty." John whispered toward us from inside.

Glancing at me with a normal smile – one which still made my heart leap a bit – Bodey moved inside. He was careful not to slam my head or my feet on the doorjamb.

We waited for John to tell us where to go next. He motioned us further into the store, while he took a few fluorescent light rods and placed them on end in front of the door. If someone touched the door, the tubes would crash to the floor – possibly shatter on impact. We would hear the noise and be alerted to any danger.

John's resourcefulness might challenge my mom's.

The moment neared when Bodey would put me down. While I didn't want to be a burden and I'm sure I was getting too heavy to carry much longer, I didn't want to lose the connection we formed in those few minutes of being close.

"Let's try in here, guys. Zero windows and one door, so if we're careful we could light a candle or something and not worry about being found out." John led the way deeper into the store.

The large cavernous center echoed our steps back to us like a large cave.

The scent of fresh paint replaced damp wood and dry needles and I breathed the change in.

Slabs of tile, granite, marble, and other material hadn't been touched in the breakdown of the world. Nothing had been disturbed – at least what we could see in the dim lighting. We could've been shopping as we walked through the interior. Well, minus the darkness, the late hour, and the lack of salesmen.

Okay, nothing about it was normal. But the ambience felt safer then outside without anything around us. That was as close to normal as I needed to be.

John closed the door behind us in the small room. We stared into the blackness, unadjusted to so much dark even after hours in the forest at night. John fumbled with his bag and after another short minute he brandished a small penlight which lit up the room with its meager beam.

A table ran the length of the wall. Stacks and stacks of carpet samples lined the side and under the counter-space. John retrieved a couple of the rectangles and shoved them under the door where the smallest crack would let even a smidgeon of light out.

Staying out of people's awareness had never made *more* sense to me before. We couldn't trust anyone. What if we came across more like Charlie or some affiliated with his group? What if the people had their own group and weren't interested in helping us but using us?

Bodey crossed to the table and set me down, allowing my feet to dangle over the edge. I slid my hands slowly down his chest as he pulled away. The texture of his jacket roughed the tips of my fingers. Disappointment must have been pretty obvious in my expression because he chuckled and chucked me under my chin with this knuckle.

Like a friend.

Double crap. For all he knew, I could be the last girl his age alive on earth and he was only giving off vibes reeking of friendship. I tucked my hands beneath my thighs and kicked my feet softly to cover my embarrassment. The movement didn't hurt when I moved my legs.

School all over again. Great.

John moved around the room purposefully, moving squares here and there into more elongated piles until they took on the shapes of —

"Beds. You're making beds, John?" I watched him, anxious for him to finish. I would love to fall asleep. I hadn't slept in for what felt like forever. I could only hold off thoughts of my mom for so long before I lost my emotional grip again. I was tired enough I wouldn't be awake long to entertain thoughts of loss and loneliness.

"I am. I'll have you over here and Bodey's is there." He pointed to opposite ends of the room. The separation wasn't lost on me, but he didn't have anything to worry about. Bodey didn't seem to think of me like *that* and it was achingly apparent.

Bodey moved to help me down, but I warded him off with an upright hand. "I'm okay, thanks. I can manage." The line came from one of Mom's old movies. Michelle Pfeiffer had amazed me and I often tried being her in one way or another growing up. I always wanted to use it.

Gingerly, I slid from the table, putting most of my weight on the uninjured leg. Hopping toward my pile of carpets, I trailed my hand along the table for stability and to maintain some semblance of dignity. Holding onto pride in that situation couldn't be more impossible, especially limping away after half-groping a boy you crushed on for an eternity.

His dad saw a problem with us sleeping near each other, but I was in no danger of being bothered by Bodey.

Dang it.

I sat on the stiff stack and stretched my legs, careful not to move my sore knee too fast. John brought my bag to my side and set it on the floor by me.

"Do either of you need to use the restroom?" John waited for our answers. I shook my head. Bodey must've too, because John sat on his pile and untied his shoes. "Let's get some sleep. I'll head out in the morning and see what I can find."

I kicked off my boots and didn't even bother doing anything with my jacket or socks. It wasn't freezing in the store, but the concrete floor – odd for a carpet vendor – wasn't putting off any heat either. Lying down, I rolled to my side and wrapped my arms around my waist. I was too tired to care and a little embarrassed. Okay, a lot embarrassed.

A slight weight covered me. I glanced over my shoulder at Bodey. He straightened a blanket over me and smiled softly before padding back to his side of the room.

Unsure what to make of his kindness and certain I was overthinking things, I gripped the edge of the blanket and pulled the soft material to my chin. The added warmth lulled me.

John turned off the light and the immediate darkness left me with nothing to think about. "G'night, you two. Get some sleep."

"Goodnight." I murmured, ignoring the tears working down my cheeks. Where had they come from?

CHAPTER 20

John tossed Bodey and me chunks of jerky from his pack. "I think it's a good thing this store hasn't been looted. It will be even better if the grocery stores haven't, but that's wishful thinking." He stuffed a strip of dry meat between his teeth.

I tore off a section of my own and chewed its unrelenting texture, grateful I had something to fill my stomach. "Thank you."

Glancing at me, John pushed to his feet. "Can you two handle being alone for a little while? I need to look around and get a feel for what we're doing here." He didn't say anything about losing his safety zone, his home base, because of me. Nothing in his mannerisms suggested anger toward me. Why wouldn't he be? I would. I knew myself enough to recognize I would definitely hold a grudge.

John slung a bag over his arm and gave us last minute instruction. "It's morning, so keep the door open in here and you should have enough light. I'll be back as soon as possible, hopefully with more food and water."

Bodey and I nodded. I yawned. Resting had been what I needed. Now when Mom crossed my thoughts I didn't spring eternal tears, only misted a little. I could handle mist. The stormy rain did me under.

Disappearing around the side of the door, John missed my grateful smile. My knee had stopped throbbing sometime during the night, but moving too fast sent sharp pain in shafts up and down my leg. Yet the injury paled because I'd slept inside and hadn't been safe in a long time.

Even with full daylight outside, the room's dim atmosphere lent a dusky kind of sensation. I blinked my eyes hard and rubbed at the corners.

I drew up my uninjured leg and leaned my cheek against the smooth part of my thigh where it met my knee. Crossing my arms around my shin, I sighed. Bodey still hadn't approached me, almost like he forgot I was there.

"So…" Great, my best line ever. How could I be so eloquent? "What I mean is, um…" Dang those ever-ready tears. They weren't because of my mom or all the stupid stuff happening or even because of the pain in my leg. I teared up because, quite simply, I had Bodey Christianson all to myself for the first time ever and I couldn't use full sentences.

He already thought of me like a sister. Why not add more to his platonic impression of me? Why not make myself out to be incompetent or slow?

I rolled my eyes and turned so my forehead rested on my knee and my tears could fall into my lap. Blowing things with Bodey compiled with the pressure of guilt over him and his dad having to leave their house, with Mom's inability to keep herself safe because of her responsibility to keep me safe, and with the loss of Jeanine who had so much more to give.

Yeah, my tears started slow and quiet, but my sobs came in like a thunderous band of bass and cellos. My shoulders shook and I dragged in deep gasps but couldn't get control of myself.

Arms encircled me. I jumped.

"Shhh. You're okay. I got you." Bodey turned me until I was cradled in his arms. He turned, lying down with me tight in his embrace, and gently pulled my face to his shoulder.

Almost against my will – except not at all – I wrapped my arms around his waist and pressed my nose into his warmth. He was solid. He was there. He wasn't dead. He wasn't even hurt.

He allowed me to cry, but my sobs lessened and I didn't feel so hopeless.

Sniffing, I turned my face to the side, resting my cheek on his chest. His heart beat thudded strong and steadfast beneath my face. If I had the guts, I could turn my head and kiss the spot where his heart was. But I had less guts than a horse fly. At least right then.

I could be blunt, but not aggressive.

"Why aren't your mom and sister with you, Bodey?" Would he notice if I traced the muscle lines under his shirt with my finger? I placed my hand on his chest opposite my face and made the smallest circles with my index finger, like it was an afterthought and I wasn't focusing my entire being on the small connection.

"They went to town for some groceries. Mom had this thing about shopping with Shayla. Girls' time, you know?" His voice came out husky and I inhaled sharp but short. Maybe he was as affected by me as I was him? Or maybe I was just allowing the hopeful sensations to crash over me, tainting everything. He made me believe better was possible.

Or it was hard for him to talk about his missing family. I understood the difficulties myself.

I lowered my gaze. "I'm sure they're making their way up…" But if they did, they would return to a burned down home and no husband or father or brother or son waiting.

Because of me.

"I'm sorry. I showed up at your place and ruined everything for you guys." Tears, again? Did I have any other way to show I was upset? Apparently, I only allowed myself to cry my way through the end of the world. I closed my eyes for a moment to stop the flow. He'd have a soaked shirt before I got off him. If I got off him.

His chest shook, a deep chuckle resonating under his ribs. "You think you ruined everything? Did you drop a particular bomb yourself or did you order this attack?"

I drew my eyebrows together, opening my eyes and tilting my head back for a glimpse of his face. "No, I mean…"

"I know what you meant. And I'm serious. This isn't your fault. Any of it. I'm glad we could help you with your mom and escape safely." His hand rubbed up and down my back, his fingers spread wide. "They're not out in that mess out there. I don't think they're… alive. But Dad… Dad gets to believe they did, okay?"

I nodded because that's what you do. "So what have you been doing? I didn't see you at track. They had the mid-season awards banquet for Coach Simpson. He retired, remember? You didn't go." My tone felt accusatory, but I wanted to know. I'd worn my favorite blue dress and had even asked Mom to braid my hair. And Bodey hadn't shown.

My finger didn't stop dancing on his chest, the small taps and twirls almost involuntary. He fought back, the warmth of his palm traced my spine. If I forgot how to talk, it'd be a small sacrifice for him to keep going.

He paused, like choosing which question to answer. "We've been hearing about a possible attack, but the one we expected wasn't scheduled for another couple months." He spoke quietly, as if the walls had ears.

"You knew this was going to happen?" Disbelief warred with my loyalty to him. "You didn't say anything to warn anyone?" How was that right?

"No, it's not like that. Everything you hear on the Circuit is rumor or needs to be treated like a possible rumor. We're not even sure who attacked this time. The one set up for this fall was actually our own government. They planned on coming in and bombing *around* all the military bases but keep the bases intact to give the appearance we didn't have anything left." He paused, letting that horror seep in, skimming my back – up and down, up and down.

"Attack their *own* country? Their own people?" The potential was unprecedented. But what if it was true? No one had fought them when they brought the stupid disease over the border – over and over and over. No one had said anything as thousands and millions had died, filling the streets. No one ever said anything – too worried about offending people.

Bodey shifted. I moved to sit up. He probably didn't want to hold me any longer. But he pulled me closer.

My eyes widened and the tingling in my skin everywhere we touched zinged like electric shock with my awareness.

"When no one sticks to their agreements and turns on each other, you don't have to stretch to see they'll even turn on themselves." He sighed, his chest heaving. "From the radio chatter we couldn't figure out who bombed who first."

"Do you know everyone bombed? Where can we go? Is anywhere safe?" What if America was the only stupid suicidal country? Bombing our own land. I never heard of any attacks or any wars on American soil in history class. But only a few years of the past in class didn't cover much except pop culture, and who cared what diva dated who when?

"No one is left. Supposedly, the governments of the countries down for a while already have small communities cropping up, but there hasn't really been a way to verify anything that we've heard." He yawned, squeezing me. "There's supposedly a series of bunkers across the country outfitted to be used as concentration camps but the government is worthless now, right? So I don't see them being used."

Concentration camps... in our country. Dad had mentioned them once or twice, but never in a good way. Why would the US have them?

I swallowed, unsettled and not only because of his hand tracing patterns over my jacket and shirt. "What do you think will happen?"

"I don't know. Dad says the best thing to do is to keep our heads down." His words disappeared as he bent and placed a kiss on my forehead. "We'll be okay. As long as Dad's with us. He knows what to do."

John was a commodity Bodey shared willingly. I didn't know if I deserved their help. I hadn't been much use to Mom and my skills weren't exactly in abundance.

What did he mean by keep our heads down? I doubted causing groups of men to chase after you failed to meet the definition.

I blew out my air. Oh, man, it was turning into a long end of the world.

CHAPTER 21

My face burned, like hot, wet lava dripped onto my skin. I know I was dreaming, but I couldn't escape. I jerked my shoulders but something held me down. I pushed and pulled. Sobs shook me. Or was that something else?

I snapped my eyes open, gulping for air.

"Kelly, you're okay. Breathe." John sat on the edge of my carpet-bed and peered at me with his penlight focused on the ceiling.

Tears streaming down my cheeks – must have been the lava – I met his gaze. "Breathing is all I've been trying to do since we left home. But I can't. I can't find…" I looked around, the tightness in my chest and throat constricting painfully. What was I missing? What couldn't I find? "Me. I can't find me. My mom's gone.

John, my whole family is gone. I have no one. Everything I do hurts someone. Hurts me." A lump formed beneath the hollow in my throat and I chewed on my cheek.

"Is that what you were dreaming about?" John's calm voice reminded me of my dad's. He always redirected my emotions, soothing me.

"No." I swiped my cheeks. Stupid tears could take a vacation any time. "We were in a group of people claiming to be our friends, but they all had guns on us. One of us was shot." I shook my head, amazed my words were even coherent. "I'm sorry, I'm not making sense."

Patting my shoulder, John spoke slowly. "You need to pay attention to your dreams. They usually tell you the route to take or teach you something you didn't know you already knew." He chuckled, the sound similar to Bodey's. "Now I sound like a fortune cookie."

I glanced at Bodey's sleeping form. "He's pretty special, you know?"

A soft smile touched John's face when he too gazed at his son. "Yep, I do know."

Trembling, I didn't want to lay down in the dark – alone – quite yet. I fingered the hem of the blanket. "What did you do before this?"

John shifted, drawing his leg up and resting his elbow on his mid-thigh. "I was a police officer. Well, first I started in the Air Force but transferred to civilian police. Dealing with the politics for a couple years, I opted out and started my own handyman business." He tapped the end of the mini-flashlight on his palm, making the beam of light dance around the room.

"Bodey told me your wife and daughter are missing." I didn't know what to say. I didn't want to be alone and I also wanted to give my condolences. I had nothing else to give.

Pressing his lips together, John stared at the floor. "I'm not sure."

My cheeks tight, I offered a teary smile. "I'm sorry. I would trade spots with them, if I could."

"No. You're more valuable than you know. Your life is just as important as theirs. If they're meant to make it, they will. We'll find each other and get this family back on track." He patted my shoulder, scooting to the edge of the stack of carpets. "I'll take care of you, Kelly. Between Bodey and me, you should be safe. We need to stick together. Get some sleep, we've had a long day."

Would it be self-serving to hope John and Bodey needed me as much as I needed them?

~~~

The hammer was harder to wield than Bodey made it look. Swinging the tool toward the nail I pinched between my fingers, I flinched. The metal head wasn't the best target and the hammer glanced off the small surface.

"Go ahead and hit that sucker hard. It's never going to go in, if you get scared. You can do this." Bodey winked at me, his face red and glistening as he struggled under the weight of the plywood board he pushed against the window hole. "Last one to get and then I can help you." He grunted, pushing harder as the board slipped in his fingers.

I closed my eyes and slammed the nail with the hammer. Thunk. I opened my eyes and squealed. "I did it!" Grinning, I admired the crooked circle as it protruded from the plywood.

Bodey stood, slowly releasing the board to the support of the tack nails. He held out his hand and I passed him the hammer. In seconds he finished placing the last of the nails and grabbed my hand as we stepped back to consider our work.

"That was the last one, right?" He wiped his forehead, releasing my hand to put the hammer on the ground by the door. We had boarded up every window in the place – which thankfully because of the warehouse status of the flooring store, only included eight across the front and a small one in back.

John had asked us to secure the place better after he scoped out the rest of the small town. The warehouse was the strongest with cement walls and double-paned windows. The only garage door access in the back was easily locked. While we did as John asked, he went out and sought necessary resources for ourselves.

Finding the plywood and pallets in the back had been a no brainer. All we had to do was put them up.

I couldn't wait for John to bring something we could eat. Even jerky would be welcomed again.

We returned to the room we dubbed the bedroom. John kept us all sleeping there because it was the safest room in the safest building in the smallest town around.

Like a kids' book.

The door opened and John walked in backwards carrying a large bucket of something. I couldn't tell what until he turned.

Firewood. We had firewood, but no fireplace. I couldn't eat wood, either. I was tempted, but the fibrous material probably wouldn't do what I needed it to.

"Where are we going to burn that, Dad?" Bodey took the bucket from John's hands while his dad stepped back outside. When he returned again, his arms full with brown paper bags, my interest piqued again.

John pushed the door closed and dropped the wood block he'd placed that morning across the jamb. "Bodey, can you grab the metal filing cabinet up front, please?"

Bodey disappeared and John turned to the wall, removing the vent cover. Sticking his head in, he glanced up and to the sides. "This should be good ventilation, here. Kelly, if you'll grab some of the paper over there, we'll get our fire going and eat something."

Eat? Did he say eat? I couldn't move fast enough. He wanted paper? I grabbed an armful of paper and rushed back to John's side. Anticipation warred with hunger. I could dig through the bags, but I had to trust John. I could do it. I could wait. I could.

I think.

Bodey returned, dragging the two-drawer metal cabinet to his dad.

John removed the drawers, emptying out the hanging folders and papers. He placed the first drawer in front of the vent which sat a few inches above the top of the drawer's height. He lined the inside with thick logs and covered those with multiple layers of aluminum foil he pulled from the bags. Then, he placed some kindling into a tight teepee in the center. He crumpled some paper and tucked the wad into the middle of that.

From his bag still on his back, he pulled a lighter. After a few moments, the pages crinkled into black leaves.

Tendrils of smoke wafted toward the vent, like it knew where it was supposed to go and couldn't wait to get out. If we could keep the fire small enough, there wouldn't be enough smoke to draw attention as it exited the building through the vast ventilation system.

While the fire worked on becoming more stable, John turned to the grocery bags and organized bags of chips, two cartons of eggs, cans of soup, cereal, rice, and cans of vegetables against the wall. "This should last a couple days while I go look for more."

"Wasn't the store looted?" Bodey retrieved our bags and handed me the dishes and silverware from mine while he handled his. John did the same and we stacked them beside the food.

"Yeah, but the Monaghans at the end of the street are still in their home. I saw Tim and we got to talking. Seems the looters hit up two of the stores, but they aren't around anymore. Two of the Monaghan kids didn't get home, but the other four are there and they're all hunkering down while they wait for the rest of their family to return." John watched the small flames, his face devoid of emotion. "We made a deal they would watch their end of town and we'd watch ours. As far as they know, no one else is around here. But…"

I waited. He had a habit of pausing while he sorted out his words. I hadn't met a smarter man, and he was deliberate, took his time, did things right. The more time I spent with him and Bodey, the more respect and gratitude I had for my situation. And them.

John sighed and looked us in the eyes, one at a time. "The Monaghans have a radio. Some of the information they've garnered includes an attack on this surrounding area because of the town of Bayview and the Naval grounds up that way. Apparently, it's a huge draw for attacks. Fairchild was obliterated during the last bombings."

Panic seized me, clenching me in its fingers. I blinked multiple times in quick succession. "You think we're going to get attacked again? When?"

Reaching out for my hands, Bodey squeezed my fingers. "It's okay. Dad's putting a plan in place. We got you."

Not for the first time did it occur to me both men were so busy reassuring me while no one worked on making them feel better. I needed more confidence in them. Start drowning my fears better.

So what if we got attacked again? Maybe surviving wasn't the best thing.

"They said tomorrow night was the best guess with all the information out there." He rubbed his eyes.

"We'll keep watch in shifts. People won't break in. At least not at first. Even if there is an attack, the chances of it being on foot are slim. The only thing that would draw people to our hideout is knowledge *we're* here. That's the appeal – they would want what we have. So we work on keeping ourselves inconspicuous. Make ourselves invisible." John chose a soup with a removable lid. "Is this okay? I figure once we eat this we can use the can to cook other things in."

Bodey and I nodded, our eyes focused on the label's picture. Yeah, we would eat that. He hadn't released my hand yet and I didn't want him to. What if John noticed? Would he regret bringing me along with him?

More importantly was Bodey being platonic? Or could that be a spark he harbored for me too? I wished I could ask my girlfriends to ask his friends to ask him.

Too much had changed. I didn't even have my phone to text him and ask if he liked me.

We waited patiently for John to put the can in the slow burning fire. Yeah, I lied. I wasn't patient at all.

Things were a lot easier with my hand in Bodey's. Even the fact we most likely were going to be attacked again was easier to deal with.

CHAPTER 22

The Monaghans were wrong. We weren't attacked the next night.

Shots started down the street soon after our soup. On my watch.

I jumped to my feet beside the AC and heating unit on the roof – the thing large enough to hide beside as we watched our perimeter.

The stars hadn't quite reached their full potential yet. Time was relative.

Flashes accompanied the shots.

Who were they shooting at?

I shimmied across the roof and slid over the edge of the access port John had found. Feeling with my foot, I found the first rung in the ladder he made out of pallets so getting up and down would be easier – even in the dark.

Another shot rang through the night.

Hand over hand I climbed down the makeshift ladder. From the bottom rung, I dropped into the room below. Forcing my fear into a compact place in my chest, I whispered loud as I darted to the bedroom. "John, someone is shooting on the north side of town." I shook his shoulder and he sat up, hand going to his waist. I never noticed a firearm there. The memory of a day when he had to protect himself constantly with a weapon had turned into his present.

Sitting up, he patted my shoulder. "Okay, get Bodey up. We need to get out of here. Inside we're sitting ducks. Outside we can go, if we need to. Grab the bags and some food and get out. I'll be lookout until you're clear." He stood, bending and shoving his blankets into his bag. He kept everything ready, like Mom had. The quality endeared me further to him.

John left the room and I turned to Bodey.

He sat up, rubbing his eyes. "I heard. Let's get our stuff."

We packed in silence. An odd tingling of déjà vu rushed over me and I swallowed back a whimper. Bodey and John weren't the only capable ones. I'd gotten my mom away from Charlie and into an empty shop safely. I could go into some woods to wait. Men weren't the only capable ones.

I could do this.

We swung our bags onto our backs. Bodey slipped his boots on and we scampered to the backdoor. John stood watch, his back to us as we closed the panel.

Bodey grabbed the straps of his bag. "Okay, Dad, we're ready. Want me to take your pack, too?"

John nodded, handing over the bag and peeking around the side of the building. He turned, pointing into the woods past the other side of the street. "Once you hit the trees, pace out fifty steps and wait for me. I'll come to you." He dug his fingers into Bodey's jacket sleeve. "Don't come back for anything, you understand?"

Bodey's eyes pierced through the dark, his jaw tight. "Yes, sir."

He reached for my hand and pulled me along beside him. More flashes lit up the street a few blocks down. John disappeared around the building. If the town was burned, like John's house, where would we go?

We reached the forest line and Bodey stopped rushing to deliberately place step after step. I followed, his hand my anchor while my stomach twisted. Each time I glanced back, I stumbled. So I focused on staying upright and looking forward.

Bodey hit fifty, suddenly stopping and pulling me to a tree where we sat down. The sound of the shots didn't reach us through the thick foliage and multiple tree trunks.

Wrapping his arm around my shoulders, Bodey pulled me close. His low voice rumbled as he worked on talking quietly but normally. Probably to keep me calm. "I remember the first time I saw you."

I pulled away from him to search his face in the moonlight. "You do?"

His eyes met mine and then he traced my face with his gaze. "Yeah. You were in your track suit and stretching. I'd never seen a girl with so much focus before. When you stood up, you brushed your hair out of your face. I wanted to help, so bad." He raised his finger and moved a stray strand from my cheek. My skin tingled.

"Why didn't you ever say anything?" I blushed. He saw me my freshman year. That was so long ago. Three years. Time we could've spent together. "I'm so embarrassed. I always had a crush on you. I thought you knew and were always just being nice." I scratched behind my ear, nervous but unwilling to take the confession back.

"What would I say? I didn't think you were interested. I didn't even go to your school." He smiled, his hand dropping to reclaim mine.

I watched him for a moment, the angles of his face softer in the shadows. "Why have you been so... friendly... since I got to your place? Like we're siblings or something?"

He huffed a slight laugh. "Can you imagine if we didn't work out? Talk about the most epic awkwardness I can think of. I'm not interested in living with the fallout, if we didn't work, you know? Or what if I revealed my feelings and you didn't feel the same? Too many variables." Bodey threaded his fingers with mine. "But... Am I wrong thinking you might feel the same? If not similar, right? This isn't a crush for me, Kelly. It never has been."

How could I be sitting here with Bodey Christianson with him asking if I feel the same way as him? He hadn't defined his feelings completely, but... if my excitement were any indication we had similar feelings for each other.

The best news I'd gotten since leaving school was finding him alive and now this? He felt the same about me all that time? My chest heaved. I was so glad I wasn't a happy crier. Finally no tears in reaction to something since leaving home.

Footsteps falling in the woods nearby drew a gasp from me. I hunkered into place beside Bodey.

I had almost leaned in and kissed him. If I died, I would regret not doing it. I turned to face him, uninterested for the briefest moment about who or what was in the woods with us.

Carefully, I placed my palm on the side of his cheek and turned him to look at me. Emboldened by the dark, the intensity of the moment, and the chance we were being hunted, I leaned toward him, closing my eyes.

Our lips met with soft uncertainty. The kiss grew with heat, as we pushed closer and more confident the other wouldn't push us away.

Another foot fall and John's voice broke us apart. "I'm off getting shot at while you two are kissing?"

Bodey and I jerked apart. I didn't know what to say. Embarrassed seemed too mild and yet, I reached euphoria with the contact with Bodey. I had liked him for so long. And he liked me, too!

I cleared my throat. "I'm sorry, John. You were shot at? I thought you were just checking things out." Stumbling over my ability to speak without sounding like a complete idiot, I couldn't make myself pull away from his son. I wasn't the type to hide my actions. John saw us kiss, my bet was holding hands wouldn't be too hard on him.

He squatted in front of us, unfazed by the lack of distance between Bodey and me. He folded his hands together, wringing them as he spoke with metered gravity. "I tried pulling the attention from the Monaghans. They'd already killed Tim and his oldest son. But they just shot at me and continued rounding up the family. We need to hide out, until they leave." He shook his head, ducking but not until after I spied a lone tear trickling down his cheek.

"Do you think we're okay here?" Bodey squeezed my fingers again. The guy had a deep desire to console me. Dang, he was so sweet.

John lifted his head, shaking off the sadness. "No. We need to find a place with more shelter. I'm not sure how long they'll be in town and we don't want to get stuck out here without any protection. I was thinking the junkyard. The old cars grouped together in the back would be good to sleep in. Any smoke from fires we could spread by fanning. I think old man Shorty even had a manual well in the back we could get some water from."

Standing, John offered me his hand. I had to let go of Bodey's to reach for it. That wasn't my favorite thing to do, but I did it. John pulled me to stand beside him and Bodey followed suit.

We followed John to Shorty's Stuff and waited while he checked out the grounds. In seconds, he returned and we followed him into the yard.

The junkyard stood sentinel on the far side of town, opposite the direction of Bayview. The exterior didn't encourage visitors with its trashed out old cars bordering its edges and towers of tossed out tires forming the fence.

Trails through piles and piles of shapes and shadows twisted and turned as we walked. I would probably never find my way out. John led us to the back, showing us the cars and pointing out separate ones for us to put our things. He was a dad, I liked that about him.

But while we waited for the world to come to its senses, how was I going to be able to kiss Bodey again with him so far away?

CHAPTER 23

Rubbing my hands together, I huddled with Bodey and John in front of the old Chevelle. The separated hood protected us from the strongest gusts of the wind. We were too far from the center of the small town to hear any gun shots. While the Monaghans had a lot of people in their family, there weren't so many members that it would take a long time to kill them all.

If the people killed the women.

My naiveté hadn't lingered long enough with Mom's experiences to believe men would simply kill women. Not when they could use them for other tasks.

"What are we going to do now?" My teeth chattered as I spoke and an involuntary shiver made me hunch my shoulders forward.

The stars disappeared and the moon faded in and out above us.

John squinted at the sky and around the yard. "To be honest, I'm hoping for rain. We'll be safe and hopefully the soldiers will move on."

"You saw soldiers? From who? Were they ours?" Bodey leaned forward, hands clenched at his sides.

John shook his head. "No, far as I could tell, they aren't ours."

"Does it matter whose they are?" I sighed. Everyone was bad by then. We were on our own. Good people were few and far between.

John nodded my way, stomping his feet. "You're right, Kelly. I don't think it does." He leaned close to us, his face inches from ours. "I need to go help the Monaghans best I can. You two stay together. If I don't come back—"

"What do you mean?" I broke in, a catch in my voice. If he didn't come back? What was this? "You don't have to go. Stay here."

John held up his hands. "Listen, getting hurt is a possibility, always. So if I don't make it back, you two need to get as close to Bayview as you can. They have a Naval submarine training site. There will be some serious militia men and they take protection very personally. You'll be looking for a Captain Simon Phahn."

He reached for both of us, gathering us into a tight embrace. A sinking feeling in my gut worried me I'd never see him again.

My brow furrowed and I clung a little longer than normal to him. He pulled back, winked at us and walked away, disappearing around a corner in the piles of junk all around us. I longed to chase him down, prevent something that I couldn't understand.

Right then, the clouds opened and rain dropped around us.

On us.

Cool drops threatened to claim every last speck of warmth. John would be getting wet, too. He needed to come back to us.

"Let's go." Bodey yanked me into the car John assigned to him.

I tucked in beside him, bringing my legs up so I could warm my hands between my knees. Watching out the window in case John changed his mind, I bit my lip. "I don't think I'm supposed to be in your car with you. I should probably be in my *own* car." Blinking at him, I held my face straight, trying not to break into laughter – even worried about his dad I couldn't help enjoying the time with him.

"I think Dad wasn't planning on this. We need to stay warm. So come here." He hauled me across his lap to land in his arms. He reached up and twirled my loose hair around his fingers. His voice husky, he watched me as he spoke. "I need to be distracted, Kelly. I'm worried about Dad. None of this is fun, you know? Besides being with you." He lifted my hand and kissed the center of my palm, slow and warm.

He had so much of his own concerns, it wouldn't be right for me to add to them. How did I tell him for the first time since Mom died, I *really* wanted to pray?

I wanted to pray because I didn't have a good feeling about his dad going to help others.

My gut instinct wouldn't reassure Bodey in any way.

So I kept my mouth shut and didn't say anything as my stomach twisted and burned more with each passing heartbeat.

~~~

Bodey's breath had evened out what seemed decades ago. I held his hand, while I was tucked under his arm against his side. Watching the rain drizzle down the windshield from the backseat, I controlled my rising panic.

I couldn't sleep. Just thinking about John and what could happen dredged up memories of Mom dying in my arms. I couldn't prevent the thoughts. Not one bit. And Jeanine running away from me. And the dog. That kid at the school. All the people.

Everyone.

Except for the people who should've been dead. Why couldn't they be gone and the good people stay around?

Closing my eyes, I slowed my breathing and pretended Mom sat next to me. What would she say? What would she do?

She'd freaking pray.

Help. Oh, help us. Please bring John back safe.

Please.

~~~

Tap. Tap. Tap.

I blinked. Smashed against the cold window, my forehead hurt. I looked up, finding John staring at me in the rainy dawn. A red streak of blood zig-zagged from his upper hairline down his forehead to his nose and cheek.

CHAPTER 24

I don't think I've ever moved so fast. Ever.

Pushing Bodey's leg off mine, I unlocked the door and shoved it open. The rain had slowed to a fine mist, sticking to my hair strands and clinging to John's beard in droplets.

"John, you're here. Are you okay? You're bleeding." I tenderly touched around the scrape which had zinged away a piece of his hair.

He moved his lips but didn't say anything. His eyes glazed over and I reached for him as he fell.

I barely caught him, oomphing to the ground with him on my forearms. Cold mud soaked my pants through to my skin. I kicked my foot on the car. Thud, thud, thud.

Screaming like I wanted to might bring negative attention and I couldn't do that to Bodey and John. I struggled to keep the majority of John's torso and head off the wet grass and mud.

Bodey peeked over the windowsill. His eyes widened and he joined us immediately in the swampy mess on his knees. "Dad! Kelley, what happened?"

"He passed out. I'm not sure before that. He tried speaking, but he fell first. Help me get him out of the cold." The chill seeped in deep, fast. I couldn't imagine how cold John was. His clothes were soaked through.

"In here. It's warmer where we were." Bodey backed into the car and pulled John while I pushed, laying him across the backseat. Bodey lowered his head, pressing his face to his dad's cheek. "What are we going to do?"

I learned from my mom. I had this.

Apply pressure.

Tearing through the bag closest to me, I handed a sock to Bodey to press to his dad's wound. "Push on his cut and hold tight. Head wounds bleed the worst."

Bad. Worse. Worst.

Because I had so much experience with that type of thing.

~~~

We took shifts holding John, checking on him. He didn't get a fever which helped me hold my stress together.

When my turn to watch him came, and Bodey slept, I cried. Flashes of Mom dying in my arms mere days ago bombarded me, overlapping his face and his weight.

Every hour we traded shifts. Minutes blurred into hours.

Bodey stepped out to scavenge some water from the well. I bent my head close to John's. "It's too soon, John. Mom already died. You can't leave us."

Shadows under his eyes frightened me further. Specks of mud spotted his pale skin.

He coughed, groaning with his eyes fluttering open. His gaze met mine, his voice caught in the fog of sleep. "Kelly? Where's Bodey?" John tried to sit up, pushing his hand to his head. "I was shot."

"You what?" I hadn't seen a bullet hole. "No, it's just a deep scratch."

"No, they shot me." He swallowed, the effort painful. "Can I have some water?"

"Bodey went to get some." I checked under his dressing, the gash not as deep looking without all the blood weeping from the lines. "Wow, this looks better. How are you feeling?"

I didn't mention the crazy fear running through me, controlling Bodey, distracting us from gathering resources or getting things checked out.

"I'm fine. I'd just run a long way and bleeding awhile." He glanced up when Bodey opened the door. A gust of moist wind blustered through the car.

"Dad, you're up." Bodey climbed into the front seat, handing over the canteen of water and smiling with relief at both John and me. He shut the door, blocking out the warmth seeking weather.

John smiled at his son, struggling to sit up on the bench seat. "I'm awake. We can go back to the store."

"What about the soldiers? Can you tell me what happened?" Bodey settled onto his heels, watching as his dad drank thirstily.

"They're gone. The group after Kelly and her mom came and they killed each other. I think the remaining members of the soldier group headed toward Bayview, so we'll stay here in Athol." He looked down at the lip of the canteen. "All of the Monaghans are gone. I…" He swallowed, avoiding our eyes. "I tried, but I couldn't save them. Not even the twelve-year-old. I forgot his name."

Bodey's eyes glistened. "What's going to happen to us, Dad?" He leaned across the back of the seat and gripped my free hand and John's shoulder.

John shrugged softly. The patter of the rain as it started up again with a vengeance broke the tension in our silence. He inhaled and then spoke slowly. "We keep surviving, son. Together. We'll do what's needed." He pulled our hands into his, holding us together in a tight group. "As long as we stay together, we'll be fine."

Stay together. Another rule I would be forced to break?

B. R. PAULSON

EPILOGUE

Six months later

We still hadn't made it to Bayview. We'd made it everywhere else in the northwest, I could've sworn to that.

I shivered, rubbing my arms briskly. Even all my layers didn't ward off the flesh freezing wind. "Three... blizzards in... two days?"

Bodey chuckled, pulling me into his arms. "I think we can call it one storm that won't stop." He turned his back to the wind, protecting me with my shoulders against a tree. The evergreen branches above held the majority of the snow at bay.

A shrill whistle reached us through the swirling snow. John waved from across the street.

He didn't yell or anything else, just that long piercing signal.

Bodey grabbed my hand and we jogged to John, our backpacks bouncing at our waists, smacking the back bones of our hips. Joining him alongside the boarded building, we huddled under the eaves of the warehouse.

"I can't believe it, but our stuff hasn't been touched since we left. We'll camp here while the weather is rough, but we won't be able to stay much past that." John pulled my pack off. He motioned us to the door. "Come on. There might still be some food in here."

I followed John and Bodey into the flooring and carpet building where we'd started out.

Six months jumping camps and scavenging for survival items took its toll.

We obsessed about food and keeping warm. The last stop before the warehouse, we camped in an old tool shed, sleeping on the dirt floor. The inside hadn't been warm enough to keep our breath from fogging.

Even though the building was cold, the biting wind couldn't reach us. I relaxed my shoulders in relief. Always fighting the elements sponged my energy. We had lost the majority of our fat stores as we fought to stay alive.

"Who do you think it was?" Someone followed us, always a step or two behind. I searched the corners, like John hadn't already conducted a thorough search. Of course he had. One thing about John – his efficiency was never half-way. He accomplished what he set out to do.

The day he decided to go after his wife and daughter, we started our trip across the northern panhandle. I've never seen such dogged persistence.

People we spoke to and traded with would give vague hints suggesting they'd seen a mother-daughter duo. We would be excited and then a new person would refute the information from before, sending us into a discouraged spiral.

Every step stung when we didn't seem any closer.

"I'm not sure who it could be. I thought for sure that gang who chased us from my place had all been killed with the soldiers at the Monaghan place, but maybe not." John kicked an empty paint can upright and slid it across to the hidden fireplace he'd made so long ago. Pulling rolls of carpet from around the setup, he squatted to the can and blew into the belly of the stove. Ash and dust clouded around him.

Tucking paper and wood chunks into the fireplace, John flicked the lighter he'd found in a previously looted gas station.

Paper caught fire fast and in minutes wood crackled under the heat of the flames.

Warmth reached me in small waves which grew steadier. I edged closer, kneeling beside John as he stared into the heat.

Bodey dropped to his rear, holding his hands up, palms out to the budding flames. "Oh, wow. That's amazing." He sighed.

Pushing at the bag he'd dropped beside the wall, John dragged three cans of corn from the top pocket. Bodey and I watched with hunger.

We hadn't eaten for two days. Water wasn't hard to come by, but food... ah, food.

I helped open the cans, meeting John's sunken in gaze. "We'll get better at this, won't we?" We'd come full circle, as if we never had left the small town of Athol, never searched for family lost in the bombs or the terror of survival. I'm not sure if we would leave that building or not, but at least we were together. At least I wasn't alone.

A genuine smile split John's somber mask. "Either we get better or we die. Nothing too serious." He winked.

Bodey chuckled and I offered a courtesy laugh.

Wouldn't it be better to die? How much more did we need to go through to reach the worst?

Hopefully this was the worst. I couldn't handle something happening to Bodey. Or his dad. I'd grown very fond of them both... okay, I couldn't lie. I was falling for Bodey and it hurt. Because what if I lost him, too? Losing someone I cared about wasn't an option. Not if I wanted to survive any longer. Losing either of them might break me.

The cost of my survival had reached an all-time high, I'm not sure I could afford the price if it rose any higher.

I took a bite and chewed the firm kernels.

Surviving wasn't the hard part. Not getting sucked in to the fear was.

I glanced at Bodey. He glanced at me and winked.

With those guys? I could survive a little longer.

THE END

of *Cost of Survival*, read further for an excerpt of Exchange Rate book #2.

Sign up for Paulson's mailing list for first time access to short stories and novellas associated with the lives of people in the Worth of Souls series and for information about other upcoming releases.

Plus, enter contests and get excerpts, shorts, and so much more that is available **only** to Survival Subscribers, please join Paulson's survival mailing list so you'll be aware of her latest releases and get all kinds of fun survival tips! Come be a **SURVIVOR**!

For a list with covers and descriptions as well as links to all of Paulson's other works please visit www.brpaulson.com.

B.R. Paulson is all about survival. Do you have what it takes to turn the page?

EXCHANGE RATE

CHAPTER 1

I'm not sure what I thought would happen when I escaped a group of men intent on selling me for resources. Hoping they'd forget about me, I didn't tell John and Bodey why Charlie and his group followed us like the most rabid of hyenas.

At least at first.

John's intuition nailed truth on the head. When he'd cornered me about the man, asking if he was the same one who'd stalked my mom and burned John's house, I'd nodded, biting back tears. My shame haunted me. We ran from Charlie while seeking John's family, using valuable energy to constantly look over our shoulders.

Even as John constantly warned us to stay together, his despondency at ever finding his wife and daughter grew. His depression worsened and more often than not he sent Bodey and me out on food hunts and resource scavenges.

"I don't want to be watch this time, Bodey." I crossed my arms and rolled my eyes toward the ceiling. John had sent us out about an hour before. I liked being alone with Bodey. His accidental touches would sometimes turn purposeful.

Ignoring me, Bodey called from inside the walk-in pantry. "Kelly, do you see anything?"

Usually I complained about it, but that's just so he'd come out and coerce me into wanting to do it.

I glanced out the window, intent on finding something – anything – to report. We needed to see some action, no matter which direction it came from. Bodey was partial to finding some food or maybe a shoot-out with Charlie and his gang. I waited for the chance to get close to Bodey, almost kiss, then kiss, and then hold hands.

The romance was helping me survive.

Food helped him.

I grinned, thinking about the different things we needed to be happy. He'd never feel about me, the way I felt about him, and I didn't care. He felt for me. Cared more than I could understand.

Caught up in my musings, I almost missed the flicker of movement on the other side of the fence. Almost. The corner of a jacket flashed red.

I jolted upright and whispered, "Bodey, someone's here. We need to go." I couldn't understand why Charlie hadn't given up. John said they'd died with some soldiers back in Athol a while back, but he hadn't stayed.

Charlie reminded me of a horrible, evil cat – more lives than anyone else around him – and he kept coming back for more. Seriously, what was wrong with the guy? We'd been running for so long, our campsites never lasted more than a day or two.

Settling had become my dream. I didn't care if things returned to the way they used to be or not. I really would like to just stay in one spot long enough to get used to sleeping in the same spot for more than two nights.

Bodey left the pantry, joining me by the window. He wrapped his arm around my waist. "Are you sure?" He peered outside, like he waited for someone to jump out with a target painted on their chest.

He thought I was trying to get him to come out to me. Unfortunately, I wasn't so tricky. I backed away from potential view. "Yes, they had a red-lined jacket on. We need to get out of here."

"You're skittish." He understood, taking my hand and pulling me toward the garage. "There's a man-door out the other side. We can hide out there until they're gone." He softly tugged me with him. I followed with no resistance.

Whoever I'd glimpsed past the fence wasn't Charlie. More brazen, Charlie walked like he owned the world and didn't care who saw him. Like we couldn't escape him.

But we always got away, even though each time our margin for success grew narrower and narrower. Sometimes, I suspected Bodey purposely tempted a brush with the man who constantly chased after me, like a protective desire to kick some butt.

The person wouldn't be John either. He wouldn't run. The jacket had been moving fast, like at a run.

I carefully closed the mudroom door to the abandoned house, shutting us in the garage. Bodey ducked through the man-door on the other side of the shop area, dragging me along. He stopped just outside the doorjamb, leaving me inside the garage. We would search our areas simultaneously while our backs were protected.

Voices carried around the side of the house, deep and male and distinctly familiar. Every time we tried getting away, they were there, like bad déjà vu. They grew louder as the men rounded the house.

Empty paint cans, broken tools, and a torn drop-cloth were piled in the corner. I held my breath, my eyes flicking from side to side as I scanned for an emergency exit. I wasn't in a movie theatre though, no neo green lights to shine the way. An upended garbage can in the middle of the cement floor testified we weren't the first ones to search that house.

Bodey glanced around sharply. He didn't wait for me to join him and instead roughly moved me outside and shoved me inside a small tool shed packed with garden hoes, shovels and other equipment. He climbed in beside me. Closing the door, he backed against the rear wall and gripped my hand in his. Short panting lifted his chest and he glanced my way, grinning.

Grinning! I narrowed my eyes. If my heart ever stopped pounding, I'd make sure to slap him on the shoulder. And if I had room, I'd lean forward and kiss the curve from his lips. Flakes of chipped pain sprinkled his dark jacket.

Footsteps fell right outside the shed. I widened my eyes.

57959256R00170

Made in the USA
Lexington, KY
28 November 2016